SURVIVOR'S AFFAIR

A JOHN LOGAN THRILLER

RICK NICHOLS

Survivor's Affair (A John Logan Thriller)

Cover Art & Design by J. Kent Holloway

ALSO BY RICK NICHOLS

THE JOHN LOGAN SERIES:

Survivor's Affair
The Affairs of Men
The Sheltering Tree
Into the Magic Night
Cold Dish
Hindsight
The Judas Man

OTHER BOOKS:

The Eastlander Chronicles

Website: www.ricknicholsonline.com

PRAISE FOR SURVIVOR'S AFFAIR

"Survivor's Affair is a whirlpool of violence, treachery, and babes who can't keep their hands off PI John Logan. Be warned, this book will suck you in and won't let go until the last shot is fired." – Sean Ellis, author of **The Shroud of Heaven.**

"John Logan joins the ranks of crime fiction's tough guys." – Simon Wood, author of **Terminated.**

"An ex-spy, turned private eye...conspiratorial twists and turns... and a murder with one heck of a sharp samurai sword. What's not to love about this book? Nichols' debut novel packs a two-fisted wallop!" – Kent Holloway, author of **Primal Thirst.**

In Japan, the legend is told of the 47 samurai whose master was betrayed and murdered by another lord, leaving them ronin—master-less samurai, disgraced and dishonored by another person's treachery. For three years, they plotted and waited until one night they struck, sneaking into the lord's castle, killing him and avenging their dead master. Legend also says that once their lord's betrayer was dead, the samurai committed seppuku—-ritual suicide—-in the castle courtyard, for they had lived only to serve something greater than themselves.

"A man's death is more the survivor's affair than his own." ~ Thomas Mann

1

"OH, GOD, HE'S DEAD..."

The voice on the phone seemed familiar to me, just on the edge of panic.

Waves lapped against the hull. A distant siren wailed across the water while darkness blanketed the houseboat. I was in bed, propped on one elbow, the phone in my hand.

"Who is this?"

"T-Tracy Rochelle...oh, God..."

"Tracy? How'd you get this num—"

"Help me, Mr. Logan..."

"Tracy, what's wrong? Where are you?"

"He's dead...holy Christ..."

"Tracy, who's dead? Where are you?"

"At the beach house."

I didn't know what she was talking about. "Give me an address."

She mumbled so I had to ask her again and wrote it down.

"Who's dead, Tracy?"

I couldn't decipher her slurred response.

"Stay there and don't do anything. I'm on my way. Are you hurt?"

The answer was faint. "No."

"Stay there, I'm on my way."

There was no response.

"Tracy? I'm coming. Stay put, all right?"

"'Kay..."

I THREW on jeans and a tee, grabbed my Glock from the nightstand, and headed out into the night.

For the record, my name is John Logan. Currently I work as a private investigator and security consultant. Before that, I was a covert operative for the United States Government. They say you never truly retire, but I did. At least I'm trying to. I did things I can't discuss in places I can't talk about and some of it I wouldn't want to even if I could. I walked away from the spy game to spend the rest of my life with the best thing that ever happened to me. Some say I became a P.I. to help people and to atone for my sins. Whatever the reason, sometimes things don't turn out the way you plan.

I was six when my parents died and I was sent to live with an uncle in Japan. When I was seventeen, he and my aunt were gunned down. At their funeral, I met a man named Bill Rochelle who said he knew my uncle. Bill took me in, brought me to America, sent me to college, got me into the military and later recruited me into the covert ops business. Tracy is his youngest daughter. The last time I'd seen her, she was a seventeen-year-old with a punk haircut and a bad attitude. I didn't know she was in the city.

How did she know I was here?

I realized I didn't know many things. Like who was dead

and why I was charging in like the cavalry at oh-dark hundred to help someone I hadn't seen in eight years?

The bay stretched out in the night, the city lights reflecting off the black water. A ribbon of steel and concrete known as the Curtis Bridge spanned the Intercoastal and connected downtown Coral Bay with the newly chartered city of Coral Beach. Traffic was light at this hour of the morning but it would still take me a half hour to get there. I picked up my cell to call nine-one-one but put it back down. I noticed the time on the phone. Three-forty-five a.m.

I suddenly knew why I was doing this. There were issues of duty and honor, lost on the average person, but not to a small number of us who'd been places and done things forever hidden from the light of day. It was a duty, not to her but to Bill, that now drove me through the night.

North Shore was an upscale section of Coral Beach that consisted of a thin strip of land between the beach and A1A and contained homes of all shapes and sizes that were worth far more than their appearance might suggest simply because of the land they sat on. I passed new half million dollar homes that bordered weathered A-frames and vacation rental houses.

After getting lost once, I found the tiny street that consisted of three houses. Tracy's was at the end on the left, right on the edge of the beach; a newer A-frame home that had not yet seen the ravages of salt and sea. I pulled into the paved driveway behind a powder blue BMW convertible. A redwood-stained porch ran around the entire house. The ocean roared, invisible from here; a light breeze brushed my face, my nostrils inhaling the salt air.

There seemed no way to get to the porch; I ran around the house, trying to locate steps but came up empty. I wondered if the architect had been drunk. There was a door, just beneath the western side of the deck. I tried the knob. It was locked. I spotted the dim light of a doorbell and pressed it. I thought about another way in and decided to hell with it. I inhaled, let the breath out and kicked the damn thing. It banged open; my Glock found its way into my hand without thought as I charged up the stairs.

I couldn't see anything in the living room except a faint ribbon of light down the hallway. My urge was to go straight to it but that could get me killed. I did a quick clear of the kitchen, then the living room. No sense being shot in the back.

"Tracy?" I moved quickly but cautiously down the hall, aware of how many times I'd done this in other places all over the globe. It never got any easier or less dangerous. The light came from beneath the closed door of the far bedroom. I went low, cursing the fact that there was little room to stand to the side of the door. If someone decided to shoot through the door, I had a good chance of being hit.

"Tracy?" I reached out, touched the knob. It was unlocked; I flung it open, went in low, pistol up and sniffing for a target.

A small table lamp shone a lone beam across the room to where I stood. The room smelled of stale sweat, sex, and booze.

Tracy sat with her back against the far wall, arms hugging her knees. Her platinum blonde hair was boyishly short. A metal stud adorned her left nostril, a T-shirt clung to her thin frame. She stared straight ahead. Streaks of mascara marked her face. I went to her.

"Tracy, are you all right? Hey kid, talk to me."

Her blue eyes met mine but held a vacant stare. The pupils were dilated. For a moment, I relaxed. She had gotten high, freaked out, and called me.

Then I looked over.

A man lay naked and face up on the bed. His mouth was drawn back from his teeth in a grimace of pain and fierce determination. He had died hard and struggling. The thirty-inch samurai sword buried in his chest had run him through all the way into the box springs, pinning the man to the bed like an insect.

2

THE FIRST TO RESPOND TO MY 911 CALL WERE A COUPLE OF uniform cops and they did it by the book. They confiscated my gun, called an ambulance for Tracy and the ME for the corpse. They took my information and let me tell my tale before sticking me in the back of a black and white.

It took only a few minutes until the beach flooded with police cars, the emergency lights illuminating the white sand in red and blue strobe effects. At least five news vans were at the end of the street. The sight made me wonder. In this city, five news crews don't show up at a murder scene at this hour unless it's someone important.

I had time to think. If I managed to luck out of this without getting locked up as the killer, then Tracy was the prime suspect. I didn't think she'd done it. She was too stoned. Or had been when I'd gotten there. I'd told her to stay quiet and make no statements until she got representation. I didn't know if she understood me. I'd have to call Bill. That wasn't something I wanted to do. Maybe the police would take care of that.

I hadn't thought to look at the sword more closely. My

guess was it was genuine. If so, it would take some skill to run it all the way through a body and into the mattress. I didn't think Tracy had that skill.

The adrenaline from earlier was wearing off and fatigue crept back in. I wanted a drink. I wanted to be back on my boat. I wanted to sleep. I sat and waited in the back of a police car and wondered who would want to kill a person with a Japanese *katana*.

I watched a man in a wrinkled gray suit come out of the house. A uniform spoke to him and pointed to the cop car that I occupied. He gave it a glance and started walking my way.

Oh, goodie.

As he got closer, I was reminded of a middle-aged Robert Mitchum. He stood about six-two and probably played linebacker in his school days. Time had softened him but he looked street tough. His blue tie was slightly askew and he had what looked to be a ketchup stain on his trouser leg. It could have been blood.

He opened the front passenger door and slid in, flashed his badge, and introduced himself. Lieutenant Jake Ross, Homicide Division, flicked the wallet closed with practiced ease and raked me over with a pair of dark brown eyes that told me he'd seen it all.

"Okay, Logan, let's have it."

"I already told the blue suits, Lieutenant."

"Humor me."

I told him the story again. He listened without interruption. When I finished, he pulled out a piece of bubble gum and popped it into his mouth, working it like a baseball player.

"Trying to quit smoking," he explained as if I cared. "Two weeks now."

"Congratulations."

"I'd sell my mother for a damn cigarette." He threw the wrapper on the ground.

"How's the girl?"

"She your sister?"

"I told you. I was a friend of her father."

"Where is he?"

"Baltimore, Maryland, the last time I heard. I haven't seen him in years."

"Must not be much a friend."

"We had a falling out."

"You have a number for him?"

"I do, assuming he hasn't moved."

"You serve with him?"

"Yes."

"Do you know who the dead guy is?"

I shook my head. "No. Should I?"

"James Forsythe."

The air seemed to leave my lungs. James Forsythe's name was on the city Trauma Center, three parks, and a boulevard. His company ranked very high in Forbes.

"You're clean with the state. Paul Jameson at the State Attorney's office says you did some work for him and you're okay, but that doesn't mean a damn thing to me."

"You don't like the State Attorney's office, Lt. Ross?"

"Nothing against them but if you're guilty you're guilty."

"But I'm not."

"Jameson also says you are an expert in several martial arts, including handling those swords."

"*Kenjutsu*, Lieutenant."

Ross sighed and rubbed his thumb and forefinger against his eyes. "Let me tell you what I have, Logan. I got the wealthiest man in this city, not to mention one of the most visible and well known, dead in a beach house with a samurai sword run through him, a half-naked girl who happens to be high as hell, and to top that all off I got a private detective in the middle of it who has the skill to use the murder weapon." He turned his head so that his eyes met mine. They were steady. Not an ounce of fear in them. "The Commissioner will be calling my Captain before this hour is up wanting to know if we've got a suspect. My Captain will ask me. The media will ask me. My office phone will ring and my home phone will ring. Every time I run to the bathroom, every reporter in the state will hound me wanting to know why we haven't caught anyone. And since this is Florida, command central for some of the most read tabloid papers, I'll be featured on them as well. Probably will say I had sex with the Yeti or some crap."

"Did you?"

He massaged his eyeballs again. "Forsythe was popular here, I think you know that. I could put you downtown and have you convicted and locked up before Forsythe's body got cold. There isn't a judge on the bench or an SA in the state wouldn't want to put their name on the list of those who helped put Forsythe's killer away."

"You don't look the type to railroad someone."

"Are you willing to bet your life on that?" He stared at me hard, reached back, and pulled out my Glock. "Permit's good and it hasn't been fired. Lab boys checked your cell phone. You got a call from the house forty-five minute ago.

"Like I said."

"I could make it, given the M.E.'s approximate time of death, that you could have done it. It would be close."

"And I killed him with a weapon I'm known to be an expert in, and left the call on my cell phone, and called the police to boot," I said. "Man, I'm smarter than I thought."

"I've met murderers who were a lot dumber than that."

"So arrest me and I'll call my lawyer."

"I don't think you have a lawyer." The tough countenance broke into a slight smirk. "There's one more thing. The girl says you didn't do it, either."

"She didn't by chance say who did do it?"

"We wouldn't have that much luck," Ross said. "It's a wonder she's that coherent."

"Do you know what she took?"

"No idea. Anything in the house?"

"Some coke and grass. Booze, of course." He snapped the gum. "How'd she hook up with Forsythe?"

"No idea, Lieutenant. Until she called me an hour ago, I hadn't seen her in eight years."

"Why'd she call you?"

"Beats the hell out of me. I didn't even know she was in town."

"Where'd she get your number?"

I shrugged. "I'm in the phone book."

"Her dad, maybe?"

"A possibility, I suppose."

Ross thought a moment. "Okay, Logan, we'll take you downtown and have you sign an affidavit for now." He got out of the car and faced the ocean. "What about the girl? The guys in there think she did it, stoned or no stoned."

"What do you think?" I asked.

Ross didn't answer me, just shut the car door and walked back toward the house. It didn't make me feel any better. I also knew it was common to fill out affidavits at the scene. Police didn't want to take you downtown unless you were a suspect.

東

THE BUILDING that housed the Homicide Division was two blocks from the beach and thirty minutes from the beach house, behind another ever-present strip mall. The building was a one-story deal with a stucco exterior and too little parking. Well groomed landscaping and clean parking signs. Nothing like impressing the tourists. You might be mugged or shot here, but at least the police building looked nice.

I sat in a tiny cold room at a worn wooden desk. Iron bolts held the furniture to the floor. The walls were institutional gray and it had a ghastly smell of fear and sweat. I finished writing and handed it over to Ross, who glanced at it.

We weren't alone. There was another cop in the room. This guy was young and probably held a college degree in psychology or criminal justice. His suit was pressed and he had the eagerness of the rookie in his eyes. I'd seen that same look from newbies in my own unit. That look would disappear soon enough.

Ross read the statement and pushed it back at me. "Sign it."

I did and he jerked his head at the door. "Okay, Logan, beat it. But stick close. I have a feeling I'll be talking to you later."

Dawn had not arrived and the houseboat was still bathed in shadows. I stepped on board and went inside. Visions of James Forsythe lying on the bed kept popping into my mind. The station coffee weighed heavy on my stomach. I reached for the bread. Some toast would be good.

Then the garrote slipped over my head.

3

WHEN DANGER THREATENS, THERE IS AN IMMEDIATE WAVE OF fear that rushes over the organism, producing a fight or flight mode. Most people choose to run away. Pros are trained to ignore the fear and fight through it.

I brought my hand up to grab the wire before it wrapped around my neck, felt it dig into my palm. The assassin pressed in behind me, pulling the wire toward the soft flesh of my neck. I reached behind me, trying to get a piece of him, but he was fast. And good. He stepped out of reach and avoided all my attempts to trip him or put him off balance. He jammed his knee into my back; an attempt to lift me off my feet. Take away my leverage and he would own me. I couldn't let him do that.

Strangling someone can be a bitch if the target knows how to make it hard on you. I used my feet to propel me backwards into him and I kept pushing, jamming our bodies together. He was smaller than I was, but he was a pro and knew what he was doing. Within a few steps, I had some momentum and was nearly running backwards. We landed on the deck together, the houseboat rocking beneath us, me on top, one hand gripping the wire, feeling the blood running down my forearm. My back was to him and still the bastard kept tugging on the wire. He knew the one axiom of the garrote: *no matter what happens, don't let go, keep tugging that wire.*

"Stop fighting, Major," he whispered into my ear. "I will make this quick."

For a split second I froze. The man knew my former rank. Not many people knew that. Either he knew me or the one that hired him did.

I couldn't find the air to say anything. With my free arm, I elbowed him in the ribs, a glancing blow that made him grunt but not enough. I fumbled around like a blind man; darkness edged into my outer field of vision. Soon it would creep closer until my brain, deprived of oxygen, would simply shut down. Panic welled in me again.

I'm not going to go that easy....

I reached between my legs. Too late, he realized what I was doing, tried to pull his legs together. When that didn't work, he twisted his lower body. The wire slid deeper into my palm, causing a new explosion of pain to slam into my hand but I couldn't stop now. I grabbed a handful of his crotch and twisted with every ounce that was in me. He yelled as the wire loosened. I turned sideways a little allowing me another inch to twist his balls some more. The wire whipped away.

I rolled onto my belly, sucking air, one hand clutching my throat. I felt the thin raised line of flesh. The bastard almost had me.

I got up to check on him. I didn't have to.

He kicked me full in the face.

I went up and back in an agonizing pirouette before twisting slightly to land face up. Stars flashed in my field of vision; I blinked to clear them away in time to see him, just a shadow towering above me. I saw the glint of gunmetal and instinctively trapped his ankle with my feet, tripping him. He went down, grunting with the impact, his gun flying from his hand. The boat rocked again causing nausea to wash over me; I managed a decent gulp of air that allowed the darkness to recede some from my vision and pulled myself up.

"To hell with it," I said, and jumped on top of him.

We grappled for a long moment for any advantage. He slipped a hand outside my guard and hammered me in the face. I blocked the next shot, punched him twice with my bleeding right hand, sending splatters of blood flying. I tried a knee to the groin but he turned away so I only managed to catch the inside of his thigh. We were half-way in the doorway to the master stateroom; there was little room to maneuver so we twisted, punched, and gouged. He was wiry and agile; he managed to get some advantage and roll me sideways, slamming my back into the door frame. He pushed away from me, diving toward his pistol near my feet. My hand couldn't reach the gun so I kicked it farther from his grasp while yanking on his shirt. The effort jerked him back and helped me up. I sucker punched him in the back of the head.

"No," I said. "You're going to earn this kill."

I clawed and scrambled, using him to get upright. I kicked him in the side and he rolled to his feet. Arms and legs flew as we attacked, blocked, trapped, and countered each other. He blocked several of my aikido traps skillfully. I slipped an arm past him, elbowed him in the face, and felt his cheek open up like a ripe melon. He twisted away and punched me in the floating ribs. My next breath hurt like hell, but I slammed him against the wall, blocked his attempt to knee me before hitting him twice more. He shoved me away and went into a crouch, holding a four-inch knife.

There is only one way to win a knife fight--control the arm holding the knife and strike with everything you have. He took a few swings at me, not wanting me to get in close. Fatigue was setting in so I waited, knowing that exhaustion would make him sloppy. He overextended his next arcing attack; I stepped inside, grabbed the knife arm, put my right hip into his belly and flipped him, held the knife arm straight as he fell, bent his wrist. I slammed the sole of my foot into his face; he brought a leg up to kick me in the back. I staggered; he rolled toward his gun. I went atop him, my hand holding his wrist back from reaching out for the gun. In that instant we froze where we were, getting our breath back, taking advantage to rest. For a moment, there was nothing except the lapping of the water against the hull and the sounds of the city. He took a deep breath and tried again for the gun. I wrenched his arm as hard as I could, took my other hand and hit the back of his head, trying to drive his face into the floor. His free hand pulled a knife from somewhere in an attempt to stab me in the face. I knew if I rolled away from the blade, he'd try for the gun realizing there was little I could do to stop him. I got to my feet and dove toward the living area, sliding over the sofa and onto the floor. I heard the muted coughing; stuffing flew from the sofa. I landed hard on my shoulder. I'd feel that tomorrow.

More bullets flew out of the sofa spraying foam and pieces of fabric into the air. I counted, hoped that I hadn't missed one. There was a pause. If I was wrong, a bullet would hit me square in the head and I'd never know that I'd screwed up.

Hell with it.

He was reloading, the clip halfway into the handle of the pistol when I came over the sofa in a tackle that caught him full frontal driving him backwards. We collided with the breakfast bar that separated the living area from the galley. He tried to maneuver his gun arm backward in order to shoot me. My fingers found my toaster on the bar and I brought it down over his head, hitting him one, two, three times with it until the pistol dropped. I drove the callused edge of my left hand into his throat; his eyes widened, mouth opening wordlessly. I got to my feet and stood over him gasping for breath as he gazed up at me, the light in his eyes fading as lack of oxygen shut down his brain. He died with his mouth open in a final effort to breathe through a throat that no longer worked.

I stared down at his body feeling something that I thought had long died. Adrenaline coursed through me, I had never felt so alive.

THE CAFÉ WAS JUST a tiny bar with several stools and half a dozen small tables around it. It served beer, hot dogs, and hamburgers and gave you a view of the walk plaza. Shops filled up three square blocks; street performers competed for the passing buck of passersby, tourists in shorts toted cameras and sunburns, and kids ran amok, testing the patience of their tired parents.

Mason Killian was six-four and two hundred plus pounds of pure Irish Texan. Together, we'd suffered through

Special Forces training and missions we couldn't talk about. He was as close to a brother as I had. He sported a blonde crew cut and mirrored sunglasses, black jeans, and a matching t-shirt with Johnny Cash on the front. Over the tee, he wore a thousand-dollar dark blue Armani jacket. He moved with catlike grace. Killian never seemed to do anything without reason. Every movement, every gesture, was an economy of motion.

"So any idea who your mystery man was?"

"No ID on him," I said, absently rubbing my neck. "Serial number was filed off the gun.

"A pro."

I pulled out my cell phone. "I took a picture. Thought maybe you might recognize him."

"Because I associate with such honorable souls," Killian glanced at the photo.

"He looked better alive."

"Not much better," Killian said and shook his head. "No bells with me, bro. Sorry." He raised a forefinger and the kid behind the counter put another draft in front of him. The kid gave an uneasy glance at Killian and hurried away.

"Where is the dearly departed?"

"Buried at sea," I said. Killian knew I didn't want the cops involved. Too many questions would be asked, some of which I couldn't answer.

"Impressive. You don't take that heap out very much."

"I just like living on it, not necessarily cruising in it."

"Apparently he didn't have a back-up."

"None that I saw." But I knew that a hired assassin would have a contact, someone that he'd report to when the deed was done. When the assassin failed to report, the other person would know something went wrong. Eventually, if they were serious, they'd try again with someone else.

I took a long swallow. "So who hired him?"

"That," Killian said, "is the big question. Who in your present life wants you dead?"

"No one that I know of."

"No disgruntled clients? No spouses of clients ticked off at you for discovering their affairs?"

"I don't do domestic cases."

"Insurance scammers mad at you?"

"This guy was too good," I said. "He didn't come cheap."

"So the client has money."

"He also called me Major. Not too many people in my current life know my old rank."

"I do."

"Did you hire him?"

"I wouldn't waste the money." Killian took another swallow. "Besides, with my luck you'd leave me the houseboat in your will. What the hell would I do with it?"

We sat in silence for a moment, each of us lost in our thoughts. We were thinking the same thing and it was a few minutes before Killian said it.

"That leaves your past life."

"I'm not in the business anymore," I said.

"They say you're never really out."

"I am."

"Okay," Killian said. "I'll play along with you if it makes you happy. I'll sit here, buy you beers and pretend that a professional hit man who sneaks onto your house-boat at five in the morning and almost kills you has no connection whatsoever to your days in intelligence. That it may have nothing to do with Shikira's death or that little escapade you pulled."

"You would have done the same thing."

"Yes," Killian said. "I would have. But you made a lot of

enemies in Washington, bro. And some of them weren't too hot on seeing you just vanish down here and become Marlowe."

"You're a pain in the ass."

"Maybe. But you're thinking the same thing I am," Killian said. "And you'd best keep your cranium from lodging in your rectum or you'll end up in the morgue."

I looked at him. "Cranium lodging in your rectum? You been reading the *Washington Post* again?"

"I'm trying to expand my vocabulary," he said. "What about the girl?"

"I think they're going to charge her with murder," I said.

"Did she do it?"

"It certainly doesn't look good for her. But my gut says no."

"What are you going to do?"

"I don't know. I should probably call Bill."

"That might be a treat."

"You have a grasp of the obvious, my Irish friend." I finished my beer and Killian lifted a finger. The kid gave me another, glanced at Killian, then left.

"Is he scared of you?"

Killian shrugged. His shoulder barely moved. "I'm such a pussycat." He downed his beer in one gulp. "You get called to a scene of a murder and then someone tries to murder you."

"You think there's a connection?"

"You're the detective, boss, I'm just the comic relief."

"What connection could there be between me and some millionaire I didn't even know?"

"Maybe none. But Tracy was with the dead guy and she's Bill's daughter and you have connections with Bill—" He spread his palms. "You see where I'm going."

"I know," I said.

"You also have another problem."

"One thing at a time, Kil."

"Got a call from Teri. She's looking for you."

I sat my mug down. "Damn."

4

I SECRETLY HOPED NO ONE WOULD ANSWER AS THE PHONE rang in my ear. Finally, I heard the click and the knot in my gut tightened a little.

"Hello?"

"It's me," I said.

There was a long pause and for a second I thought Bill Rochelle would hang up. "This is a surprise."

"I know. Look, I'm sorry for bothering you but I wanted to tell you about Tracy."

Another pause, then: "What's she done now?"

"She's been arrested for murder." I told him the whole sordid story.

"And what do you want me to do about it?"

"She didn't do it."

"Okay."

"I just thought you'd want to know, maybe see about a good attorney or—"

"I can't help her, son. She and I haven't spoken in years. Last time she told me to eff off, so I did."

"I'm sorry, sir. I didn't know."

"I gave her your number just in case she got into a jam. I guess she did." His voice was low. "I heard about your little mission. You should have called me."

"I didn't want to get you involved," I said. Now came the moment. "Bill, I need a favor."

No response.

"Someone tried to kill me last night. Professional. No I.D. on him, he knew my rank. Maybe you could use your connections and see if anything's been issued on me."

More silence.

"Bill, dammit, talk to me."

"We'll talk," he said. "But not on the phone. I'll find you. Watch your ass, son." The line went dead as I stood there clutching the phone.

THE ROOM WAS RECTANGULAR, longer than it was wide and composed of narrow wooden strips held together by glue or pieces of wood. Not a metal nail in sight. The floor was worn from years of use.

His name was Kenosha. He'd been the owner and sensei of this dojo for ten years. Short and powerfully built, he stood in front of me, the six-foot staff held before him in an easy one-hand grip. His skill was deceptive due to wire rim glasses that made him look like a college professor, which in fact he was. He taught Asian history at the university when he wasn't busy trying to kick his students across the floor.

I waited, unarmed.

I felt it more than I saw it. Without warning, Kenosha brought the staff down in a diagonal slash toward my head. I rolled away, coming up on one knee to raise my arms, crossing my wrists to block the next strike before rolling again. Once, twice, three more times, he attacked, the staff whirring so close to me that I could feel the wind of its passing. I moved and blocked by pure instinctive training. If I'd taken the time to think about it, I would have been knocked unconscious.

He tried an overhead strike and I rolled away again, grabbing the other staff that lay on the floor. I succeeded in getting as far as a kneeling position when he performed another overhead strike I barely managed to parry. The tip of his staff stopped a hair from my skull. I rolled to my feet, trying for a side strike, which he parried with a vertical block.

Our staves made a loud *clack clack* as they struck each other in the relative quiet of the late afternoon. I hadn't practiced *bojutsu* in a while and I think that's why Kenosha wanted to do it. Sweat covered my chest, ran down my sides, soaked the tee shirt beneath my *gi* jacket. I suddenly went to one knee, my staff flashing out in a sweeping movement that Kenosha barely managed to jump; while in the air, he powered his own staff down like a baseball bat in a strike at my head. I couldn't block it in time and had to roll away, again coming to my feet.

Kenosha was relentless today. I couldn't seem to get on the offensive and I knew it was because my lack of practice and concentration. My mind wasn't fully into it and I'd been lucky to have lasted this long. I did a knee strike, the tip of my staff catching him on the back of the leg. I heard him grunt with the effort. We spun at the same time and ended up in a draw, the tips of our *bo* an inch from each other's chin.

We stepped back, bowed. Sweat dripping from me, I walked off the floor thinking how closely I'd come to defeat.

東

"YOU SEEM PREOCCUPIED," Kenosha said as we knelt in his office for tea. The floor was covered in *tatami* mats; there was a gap between his and mine, the space between host and guest, always observed. He whisked the green tea into a nice froth and poured it into the ceramic cups. He handed one to me and I took it, feeling the warmth in my palms. I put the cup to my lips, tasted the hot bitter liquid and was reminded of all things good that was Japan.

"Your mind was not quite on the match," he said.

"I have something on my mind."

Kenosha took a sip of his tea. He was a picture of calm and harmony.

"Someone tried to kill me yesterday." I related the basic story.

"It is not the first time you've been in danger, given your background."

"True," I said. "What bothers me is the man was a professional. Someone paid him a lot of money. I'm afraid it might have something to do with my past."

Kenosha sighed softly. "You mean your days as an operative."

"I gave that life up."

"Perhaps, but you cannot erase it. What you were then is what you were and there are ghosts that sometimes refuse to go away." He sat his cup down. "You can walk away from the life, John, and try to become someone else, but you will always retain some of what you were. Once you accept it, you will find the peace that now eludes you."

"I haven't had peace since she died."

"I know." My sensei sipped more tea. "You felt the need to avenge her and you did. At quite a risk to yourself."

"They killed her, sensei. Trying to get to me. I could not do otherwise."

"It is not for me to say," he retorted. "You did what you felt was right."

"So what do I do now?"

"You know what you need to do. Ignoring your past will not solve your current problem. You will need to address the situation."

"It might require me..."

He nodded. "To become the person you used to be."

"Yes."

Kenosha was quiet for a moment. "On your boat, during the fight with the assassin. What did you feel?"

"Fear, anger. The adrenaline of battle, of course."

"All normal primitive emotions."

"There was something else," I said. "When I killed him. I felt..." I struggled to find the word.

"Like you used to feel when you killed."

"Yes."

He nodded. "You felt the old feeling, the operative standing there doing battle with this man, no longer a private detective living a quiet life."

"It scared me."

"You've been trained in martial arts since you were six. Plus, there is your military training, the schools of covert training. Survival is ingrained into your brain and body—indeed, your very soul. You cannot change that. When the threat reared its head, your body did what it had been trained to do, automatically. You should know this. Do we not strive for that very thing in the dojo? To make your body respond automatically, without conscious thought?"

He was right. "I could have knocked him out, disabled him," I said. "But I didn't."

"No. You did what you were trained to do."

"I know," I said. "But the feeling was overwhelming. I hadn't felt that way in a while."

"Your body responded. You were alive and he was dead. The organism rejoices in it."

"I cannot change it, can I?"

Kenosha rose to his feet. "No. You told me when you first came here about your first *sensei* in Japan, *Sensei* Funichi. What did he say when he first met you, when you were six?"

"He said I had an old soul. A warrior's soul."

"And that is what you will always be at heart," Kenosha said. "Come. We still have more practice to do."

5

The law offices of Karen Lords were on the tenth floor of the Bank of America Building. The lobby had a large picture window on the back wall that gave a breath-taking view of the Bay. The receptionist led me to Karen's office and offered me coffee or water. I chose water. The chair was so comfortable I could sleep in it. I looked across the mahogany desk at the middle-aged woman behind it. Karen had dark brown eyes and she used them to bore holes in me.

"Thank you for coming, Mr. Logan. I admit I haven't heard of you."

"I've heard a few things about you."

"Probably not all good."

"But not all bad, either."

She smiled. "Either one was probably true."

"I'm sure. What can I do for you?"

"My friends at the State Attorney's office say you're a good detective."

"I wouldn't think you'd have any friends there."

The receptionist returned, handing me the water. Karen

thanked her and the receptionist closed the door as she strode out.

Karen smiled. "One or two. And they say you're good."

"I have a good publicist."

"Are you always so…"

"Witty?"

"That wasn't my first choice of words."

"Smart ass?"

"That would do," she said with another smile. Karen had dyed auburn hair and full lips. There were small lines around her mouth and eyes. Her skin was brown and lightly freckled from years of sunbathing. Her legs were still nice and it was obvious that she worked out a lot. She could still turn a few heads.

"Most of the time," I answered. "Sometimes I'm worse."

"Good. So am I." She turned her attention to the file on her desk. "You have a problem."

I leaned farther back in my chair and took a drink of the water. I didn't say anything.

"The Rochelle girl has been arrested for murder."

"I don't think she did it."

Karen nodded. "That's why I want you."

"You want to hire me?"

"Jim Forsythe was a well-loved city figure. He was also an ass of the first level. I know—-I met him a few times." She leaned back. "You ever meet him?"

"No. We never traveled in the same circle."

"He was the horniest man I'd ever met. I did some work for him once and he would often come by and shamelessly proposition my receptionists."

"Sounds like grounds for a sexual harassment suit."

She snorted. "Good luck suing Jim Forsythe for anything. The man had a battalion of excellent attorneys working for his company and a dozen more slobbering at the chance to represent him. You're one of the few people I've crossed who hasn't hung my client out to dry."

"You're representing Tracy?"

"Yes, as of this morning."

"May I ask why?"

"Why wouldn't I?"

"Given Forsythe's reputation, I would think most of the defense attorneys in the city wouldn't touch Tracy's case."

"I'm not them," she said.

"Does that include your reasons for wanting me on board?"

"I have two reasons. One, because you have a reputation as being a tenacious investigator. Two, I received a call from Tracy's father. He recommended you."

"Did he hire you?"

"No. I'm doing this *pro bono*."

"But the publicity it will generate, especially if you win, would be worth more in the long run, right?"

She nodded in agreement. "You and I believe the same thing: that Tracy Rochelle is innocent. And I do believe that, Logan. I really do."

"A defense attorney one time told me that he didn't care about his client's guilt or innocence. He worked to get the client acquitted, whatever the circumstance."

"Hence your dislike of my profession," Karen said.

"Not dislike. More like a mistrust."

"I admit there are a lot of attorney's out there with that attitude," Karen agreed. "I'm not one of them. If I thought Tracy was truly guilty, I wouldn't touch Forsythe with a ten foot pole unless her father coughed up some huge money."

"She didn't kill him," I said.

"What makes you so sure? What happened that night?"

I told her. When I finished she scribbled something in the file. "That doesn't look good for you, either."

"Tell me about it."

"Did you kill him, Mr. Logan?"

"No."

"So far the telephone call is your one thin point of grace."

"One more thing: Tracy said I didn't do it."

"And I could destroy that statement in a courtroom very easily," she said. "Tracy was stoned when they picked her up. Her statements made during that time could be called into question. The prosecutor is probably not losing sleep over that one. I wouldn't be."

I shrugged. "If this is a problem for you, I understand. Find yourself another detective."

"No. I want you."

"Okay." I offered. "I leave the legal business to you; you let me do my job."

"Agreed. Now is everything agreed to so that we can get on with this damn thing?"

"It works for me, counselor."

Calmness settled around us for a moment. A truce and an understanding had been reached. Now we could move on.

"What do you charge?"

I told her and she didn't flinch. "Fine."

"Can you afford me?"

"If you can prove Tracy's innocence, I'd better damn well afford you." Karen pulled out an envelope and handed it to me. There was a check inside.

"A retainer," she said. "So, what do you do first?"

"Basic stuff. Find out everything I can about Forsythe

and his business. Sift through it and see if there is anybody who'd want him dead."

"Do you think it will get you anywhere?"

"You don't get to be James Forsythe without making a few enemies along the way," I answered. "Let's see whose hit list he was on."

"Okay."

"I'm also going to need to talk to Tracy. I want to know what happened at the house that night."

"She's already made a statement."

"What did she say?"

Karen handed me the file. The statement was straightforward. Forsythe had scheduled a business engagement that night. Tracy stated that an older man had shown up with a young woman that she assumed to be a high-class call girl. She had been introduced to Tracy as Amber. So far, there was no sign of her. Tracy didn't know who the man was. He'd been introduced only as Frank. She'd given a vague description but it was of little value. The four had dinner, then Tracy and Amber started the after party festivities. Tracy stated that she went to the bathroom to "do a line," and when she got back, Jim was dead and Frank and Amber had left. But she couldn't remember if they had gone prior to her going into the bathroom.

I finished the statement and looked over at Karen. She seemed to read my mind.

"Weak isn't it?"

"Thin as paper," I said. "You got your work cut out for you."

"So do you," she said.

TRACY SAT across from me in an orange jumpsuit. Her eyes were sunken and vacant; it would take a lot of sleep to erase the exhaustion that lay behind them. Karen sat beside me.

I asked, "How are you doing?"

Her voice was almost robotic. "You came to see me."

"Of course. How are you feeling?"

"Okay. They say I've got to go to detox."

"Yes, they told me that, too."

"It's gonna be bad, samurai." That was her nickname for me since she'd learned as a kid that I'd been raised in Japan.

"You can make it. You're tough."

"No," she said. "No, I'm not."

"I need you to be strong, Tracy. You're in a lot of trouble."

She stared at me. "They say I killed him."

"I know. I'm going to try and prove you didn't."

"Can you do that?"

"I'm a private investigator now, Tracy. I'm going to try. So is Karen. But we need your help."

She didn't seem to hear me. She didn't respond.

"Tracy? I need your help, okay?"

"'Kay," she mumbled.

"Tell me what happened that night. The night Jim was killed."

"I told the police."

"Tell me. Sometimes you remember things after awhile. Tell me what exactly happened."

"It's too hard."

"Trace, come on, I need to know."

She took a deep breath. "Jim called me and said that we were having a small dinner party for two guests. That was his way of saying that he was having someone important over and that I was expected to be there for him and the guests." She closed her eyes. "Jim came over to the house first."

"Does he own the house?"

"Yes, it's in one of his company's names."

"Okay. What time did Jim arrive?"

"About six, I guess. He brought the food with him; nothing fancy, just subs and finger sandwiches. Light stuff."

"What else?"

"About seven a couple arrived. The guy was older. He kinda looked familiar but I'm not sure."

"How do you mean?"

"I don't know. Like I saw him somewhere. TV or something. Jim said his name was Frank."

"No last name?"

She barely shook her head. "No."

"What did he look like?"

"Older. Probably fifties. Needed to lose some weight."

"How was he dressed?"

"Slacks and a polo shirt. Nothing fancy."

"Okay, what about the girl?"

"Amber. Young, about twenty-two or so, blonde like me. Pretty. She was a call girl."

"How do you know that?"

"When you've been one, it's easy to spot another one. Besides, she told me."

"She from around here?"

"I don't know. I don't think so."

The rest of her story was true to her statement. They had eaten and Forsythe and Frank had spent awhile talking in private. Tracy didn't know about what. Business, she supposed.

"Okay, then what?"

"Jim came out and whispered that Amber and I needed

to liven up the party. That was his little hint to me that things were going to get wild. So Amber and I started fooling around on the couch in the stateroom while the guys watched and talked. Jim made sure that this Frank got involved and we did him in the bedroom. Afterward, he talked to Jim some more and left. Amber stayed for a while and the three of us...had sex for a while. I ended up falling asleep. When I woke up Amber was gone. Jim and I made love again and then I went to the bathroom. There was some coke on the counter so I did some and came back out. Jim was dead." She lowered her eyes.

"You didn't see anyone? Hear anything?"

"No." Her hands were shaking and I noticed beads of sweat on her forehead. She was coming apart.

"How long were you in the bathroom?"

"I-I don't know..."

"Tracy, you hang in there, okay? I'm going to get you out of this. But you have to get clean and be strong for me."

Her eyes shut tight and she wrapped her arms around herself. "I'm scared, samurai."

"I know. Do you want me to call anyone?"

"No."

I wanted to hold her, to take her and give her the reassurance that it would be okay but physical contact with her was forbidden. "It's okay, Tracy. You just go and get straightened up and get some rest. Samurai is on the job."

She raised her head. For a moment, the frightened child was gone and the street tough girl was back. "Daddy always said you were the best he ever trained. Was that the truth or was it all bullshit?"

I've wondered that myself, I thought.

"I'm going to get you out of this, Tracy. You just do your part, okay?"

She gave me a nod and I motioned for the guard. I caught a fleeting glimpse of her orange jumpsuit as they led her away.

"What do you think?" Karen asked me.

"What about bail?"

"I'm not hopeful."

I sighed. We weren't getting any breaks. "I think she's in for a rough road. Have the cops uncovered anything else?"

"Not really. They're treating this case as finished with Tracy's arrest. Logan, you have to get me something. Otherwise she's going to death row."

THERE ARE simple ways to know if someone's been in your house. My favorite is the thin strand of monofilament line stretched across the door and the frame. When someone opens the door, the line breaks. Therefore, you know that someone's been there. The line was intact and I went inside. I made a tuna sandwich, grabbed a beer, and went out onto the deck.

Tracy was in a lot of trouble. There were various avenues to pursue. One was to investigate James Forsythe. Another was to try to find Amber. Whoever she was, she would be hard to find even if she were local, but easier than if she were from out of town. The mysterious Frank would prove even more difficult. I had nothing on him but a vague description. No idea who he was or what he did for a living.

They arrived an hour later. I watched them get out of the car and walk down the pier. The man looked to be just out of college and dressed in a dark suit, the woman was older and not bad looking. She had on black slacks and a matching blazer over a white blouse. Her hair was a subdued red, straight and brushed to her collar.

"Mr. Logan?" She flashed her badge. "I'm Special Agent Healey and this is Special Agent Barlow, FBI. May we come aboard?"

I nodded and Healey stepped on deck with ease. Barlow, the guy, did it a little more gingerly. He wasn't used to boats.

"Did we catch you at a bad time?"

I had changed into swim trunks and a tank top and was scraping rust off the foredeck railing. "Something tells me if I say yes, it won't matter."

"We were told you didn't like the Bureau," Barlow said.

"Not true. I have nothing against the Bureau. Just some of the people who work for it," I stated. "Now if you'll forgive me, I'd like to get this railing scraped and painted before it gets too dark. What can I do for you?"

"You talked to Bill Rochelle recently."

"Yes."

Barlow found a chair and sat down. "Bill Rochelle's daughter was arrested last night. The police took a statement from you."

"That's right."

"How are you involved in this?"

"Bill's daughter called me. She was scared and I went to help her. I didn't know anything about a body until I got to the beach house."

"Why did she call you?"

"Because I know her father and I was closer than he was."

"Are you sure?"

"She was scared, panicky, and high," A piece of rust

wouldn't budge and I put a little extra effort trying to get it loose. "What's all of this about?"

A faint smile tugged at Barlow's mouth. "They're going to charge her with murder."

"I know. I've been hired as a defense investigator. I don't think she did it."

"Why did you call General Rochelle?"

"To tell him about his daughter," I said. "I thought he might like to know." I got up and Barlow tensed until I sat down in a deck chair. Maybe it was my imagination but I thought Healey's eyes quickly raked over me.

"Anything else?" Healey said.

There was no need to tell them about the assassin. "Should there be?"

Barlow dropped the smile, "General Rochelle was murdered last night in his home."

6

THE LAST TIME I HAD SEEN BILL WAS FIVE YEARS AGO—THE day I resigned. He'd sat behind his desk staring out the window that overlooked DuPont Circle.

Major General William Rochelle, US Army retired, had been given the nickname "The Rock" in Vietnam for his efforts in helping to evacuate his men during a firefight on some forgotten hill near the Laotian border. Bill had single-handedly held off a platoon of VC regulars buying time to get his men aboard the choppers. Shot twice, he was still firing when he'd climbed aboard the last helicopter. That incident had earned him the moniker and a Congressional Medal of Honor.

Five years. A lifetime it seemed. I'd stood at attention in front of his desk and he made me sit.

"Are you sure about this?" He was still looking out the window.

"I am."

He swiveled around; those damnably clear gray eyes bore into mine. "You're making a mistake, John."

"I've had enough, Bill. I want a normal life."

He chuckled. "Normal? A man like you can't do normal. You want to know why? You're a soldier, a killer. You're the best I ever trained and you want to throw it all away to be with Shikira and have your white picket fence and your two car garage?" He slowly shook his head. "You'll be bored in a month."

"She means everything to me, Bill. I'm not going to let her go."

"John, you're throwing away a lifetime of training and service over a woman?"

"She's not just any woman, Bill."

"Your country needs you. I need you."

"I want to believe that," I retorted. "In the end what good are we doing? Don't think I don't know about the pressures Capitol Hill is putting on you. We're not PC anymore, Bill. We're not supposed to go out and kill America's enemies. We're supposed to let them screw us."

Bill leaned back. "Is this about South America?"

I took a deep breath.

"That's what this is all about," Bill said. "Look, John, I'm not blaming you for that. It wasn't your fault."

I'd told myself that on many nights since and it hadn't worked.

"Don't let this one bad thing ruin you. We can rebuild the team again."

"They're not going to let you, Bill; you and I both know it."

He waved it aside. "Just politics, John. Old Senators spouting tough talk. They know, as we do, America still needs us."

"Maybe. But not with me. I'm done."

For a moment I saw the pain in his eyes. "Don't do this, John. I'm begging you."

"I'm sorry, Bill," I got to my feet. "I just don't want to do this anymore."

I saluted but he stuck out his hand and I grasped it. I thought I saw tears in his eyes.

"Okay," he said.

"Bill—"

"You're dismissed, Major."

I straightened, did an about-face, and walked out.

Now, sitting on my boat and hearing Barlow's words, it seemed as though my brain refused to process them, as though there was some sort of error message.

"Murdered? How?"

"Sniper," Barlow said. "Waiting in the trees just on the perimeter of the estate where they could look on the east side of the house where the pool was. Rochelle apparently was talking to someone on the phone and walked to the doors. M.E. says he was dead when he hit the floor. About 150 yards. Pretty easy shot for any sniper."

"Any leads?"

"None. As you probably know, the Rochelle house was enclosed by a high stone wall. We think the killer parked along the adjacent street and climbed over the eastside wall. He'd have his best cover and line of fire there."

"So why are you here again?"

"You called him. I suppose you two have kept in touch."

"Quite the opposite. Until I called him, I hadn't talked to Bill in three years, five years since I've seen him."

"Before this week, when did you last talk to him?"

"You're not listening, Agent Barlow. Three years. I called him on the day he retired."

"You two were close."

"Once. He was a surrogate father to me. We had a bit of a falling out."

"May I ask why?"

"No," I said. "It was for personal reasons, not professional."

"You left government service and came here with your wife, I believe," Barlow said. "Did you two split up?"

"She died last year."

"I'm sorry," Barlow said reflexively. He didn't mean it. He didn't care. It was one of those things that you say to keep from looking like a cold-hearted ass.

"So why did you call Rochelle last night?"

"To let him know about Tracy. Nothing more."

Healey had been quiet for a while. "Did Tracy get along with her dad?"

I shrugged. "She's always been a bit of a prodigal. Bill used to have fits over her antics."

"What kind of antics?"

"Not sure. Bill kept it pretty close to the vest, but I know she used to run away a lot, started drinking at an early age."

"Drugs?"

"I don't know about then but she was pretty whacked out the other night."

"Okay, Logan," Barlow got up. "We'll be in touch if we have any more questions."

"Let me know first," I said. "I'll make coffee."

I watched them walk down the pier and drive away. Only after they were gone did I feel the hot sting of tears before I angrily blinked them away.

I owed a lot to Bill. He'd taken a scared teenager and gave him security and direction. When I needed advice, Bill had always been there. When I would come to his home, I was treated like a son. That last conversation had been about Tracy but I also believed that maybe it had been a prelude to healing old wounds. I would never know.

I went inside and grabbed a bottle of Crown Royal from the galley. I sat watching the waters of the bay, blue and sparkling in the afternoon sun.

We need to meet. Watch your ass, son.

Bill knew something was going on. He couldn't tell me over the phone so he wanted to meet in person. He also told me to be careful. That meant I was still in danger.

Whatever Bill knew, it had cost him his life. Now his daughter sat accused of murder. I couldn't help Bill. Maybe, with a little luck, I might be able to help his daughter.

CHARLIE'S WAS A CITY INSTITUTION. Located on the beach in a two-story frame building, the bar and grille served the coldest beer, the hottest wings, and the best steak in town. Inside, the walls were decorated with military memorabilia from America's wars; over the bar was a large framed copy of raising Old Glory on Iwo Jima.

There really was a Charlie. He was a bulky man with a Hemingway beard and a Marine Corps tattoo on his thick forearm. He had a scar on his temple from a VC bayonet when he was a young corporal in a war nobody wanted.

"Meeting someone, Charlie," I said to him when I walked up to the bar. "I need someplace out of the way."

He nodded and motioned to the rear section of the restaurant. The hostess showed me a cozy table that overlooked the beach. The Atlantic kept rolling in, the waves low much to the disappointment of the surfers.

Dana Costello was a local reporter who never made me

nauseous when she was doing one of her infamous investigative reports. She had a reputation as a fair and honest reporter who loved her job and didn't buy into the hype that seemed to swirl around the more well-known anchors. She had the looks to be an anchor and certainly had the brains. But she didn't want it until she wanted it. And she didn't want it. As she once said to me over a few beers, she was having too much fun making city government squirm.

Now she was in jeans and a tank top that showed off her curves. She had brown hair and matching eyes and a smile made for television. She gave me a hug and a peck on the cheek and, when the waitress showed up, ordered a club soda. She'd been sober two years now.

"I'm glad to hear from you. It's been a while."

"Sorry. I've been trying to keep it together," I said. "How have you been?"

"Good. Janice moved in with me. So far, it's going well. This is the longest relationship I've had in years."

"Good. I'm happy for you."

"How about you?"

"I'm okay." I sipped a soda.

"You don't sound convincing."

"Sorry."

"Time will heal, John."

"So they say."

"Are you dating?"

"Not really interested, really."

"It'll happen," Dana said.

"Maybe. What do you have?"

"Uh-oh, quick change of subject," she said. "Are you sure you want to do this? We are talking Forsythe here."

"Yes."

She told me what she knew. James Forsythe was a local

hero, philanthropist, and near-god to many of the city folk. He was a local boy who'd lived a Dickens rags-to-riches life. He owned one of the largest investment companies in the state and half of the city parks and recreational areas were there because of him. The state-of-the-art trauma center at University Medical Center bears his name. He had always been prime fodder for the local gossips. He was married, two grown kids.

"What about his reputation as a playboy?"

The waitress brought her club soda and smiled when she recognized Dana. Dana took a sip and thought a moment. "The womanizing is reputable enough and there have been rumors that he was actually a sex addict. There was an incident in Palm Beach a few years back that nearly broke the dam open. Forsythe was allegedly screwing the seventeen-year-old daughter of a socialite down there and the mom found out. A reporter for the *Miami Herald* broke the story but it never made print. The story got killed right out of the starting block and rumors were that it was Mrs. Forsythe herself that killed it."

"Why would she do that?"

"Emily Forsythe uses her husband's name to raise money for over two dozen charities. She probably would like to keep his name unscarred."

"What else?"

Dana shrugged. "He liked them between seventeen and thirty. His yacht, *The Golden Egg* is rumored to be one of his party places. You ever meet him?"

"No."

"Rich, intelligent, and damn good looking," Dana said. "He'd make me consider going straight."

"What would Janice say?"

"Hey, if I got rich out of the deal, she might forgive me."

"What about his company?"

"The Forsythe Group is a conglomerate now. They own mining in Brazil and diamonds in South Africa. They have a lot of hands in a lot of things. They are currently working on a deal to buy a small overseas company called MicroCorp. Word has it that their R&D department would be a great asset to Forsythe's electronics division."

"What about Mrs. Forsythe? Does she ever get tired of her husband's wanderings?"

Dana said, "Emily Forsythe is from a blue collar Chicago factory worker who worked his ass off to get her to Dartmouth where she majored in Business." She took another drink, checked her notes. "She met her future husband right after graduation and they have two kids—a boy who is in his senior year at Yale, and a girl who is in med school in Ohio. Quite a success story. Word has it that Emily puts up with her husband's dalliances as long as he's discreet. She stays for the money, the prestige, and of course her charity work."

"The trophy wife," I said. "She could kill him in divorce court."

"Probably, but it would cost her a couple of positions on certain boards and charities. She likes that. Besides..." Dana wagged a finger at me. "Don't let the obedient wife act fool you. She is every bit as tough and tenacious as her husband. She is keen on keeping the Forsythe name in good standing, despite her husband's attempts to ruin it at times." Dana sipped her soda. "So why are you asking?"

"I'm helping the defense."

"You're trying to prove the Rochelle girl innocent?" Dana asked. "You have your work cut out for you."

"I know. She didn't do it, Dana."

"Let me tell you something, John, the Forsythes are not to be messed with. You start dabbling in their affairs and they will cut you in half. The only thing they hate more than nosy reporters is nosy PI's."

"I'll keep that in mind."

"You do that," Dana said. "Is there a scoop here?"

"I don't see one yet. If I can prove she's innocent, yes. I'll let you know."

"Okay. By the way, I was in Miami recently doing some research on a story. I spotted one of your wife's paintings in a shop there. Owner bought it from one of her shows."

"Do you remember which one?"

"It was the bay at sunset. It was so real you felt as though you could reach out and touch it."

"I remember that one. She had a fit trying to get it just right."

Dana said. "I miss her."

"Everyone who knew her misses her."

Dana glanced at her watch. "Sorry. Have to run." She got up and kissed me on the cheek. "Watch yourself, John."

7

"YOU'RE A HARD MAN TO FIND."

I was on the foredeck, sitting at a table looking through the stacks of information I'd collected on James Forsythe when the voice made me look up.

Her dark blonde hair was longer and curlier than I remembered, but otherwise Teri Johnson looked the same. The legs were still long, the waist narrow, the curves toned, the lips full and sensuous. She wore jeans and a spaghetti strap top. Ray-ban sunglasses hid her hazel eyes. Men would give her more than one glance, but there was also a sensuousness about her, a sexuality that went beyond mere appearances. Many girls are pretty and nothing more. They're the kind that you look at twice and move on down the street. A woman like Teri will stay with you, the memory of her movements lingering in your mind. She will haunt your dreams, her expressions playing over and over like a song to which you can't stop listening. I felt something stir in my gut; a knot I thought long dead. For a moment, I could only stare. I think I stopped breathing.

"This is a surprise."

She gave the houseboat a quick appraisal. "Is this thing sea worthy?"

"It's floating, isn't it? Come aboard."

She stepped on with the grace of a Vassar girl. I got up and went to her. She surprised me by embracing me hard, her arms around my neck. "Bill's dead."

There was the whiff of her strawberry shampoo, her breasts pressing into my chest, the firm slim waist beneath my palm. Holding her, the years disappeared in a flash and memories of another time came flooding back to crowd out all the reasons why we had walked away from it.

"I know," I said. "I heard."

She stepped back, arms on my shoulders, and smiled. "You look good."

"You, too. It's been a long time."

"Mason told me about...Shikira. I'm very sorry." Teri was the only one I knew who called Killian by his given name.

"Thanks. Would you like a beer?"

"Bottled?"

"Of course."

A nod. "I'd love one."

I got one from a cooler on the deck and handed it to her. She took a seat and gazed over the water. "I like the view."

"Water has always calmed me."

"I know," she said. "You lived somewhere else before?"

"We had a house near the beach. When she died, I couldn't stay there. I sold it and bought this. It's enough for me."

Teri's face darkened. "We have to talk.".

"I've got a lot on my plate right now."

"Bill isn't the only one who's ended up dead," Teri said. "Several members of the unit have died over the last six months."

That got my attention. "Who?"

"Taylor, Wilson, Addison. You remember Addison?"

"Never worked with him, but I remember him."

Teri nodded. "Gina was the latest."

I remembered Gina Kennedy. She had been under my command at one point.

"How?"

"She was working in L.A. We talked once in awhile. Someone broke into her high security condo and drowned her in her bathtub. Shot her full of heroin to make it look accidental. I told the police that Gina wasn't a user but no one listened." Teri took a large swallow of beer. "She fought hard, John."

"Jesus," I felt as though the wind had been suddenly knocked from my body. "Now Bill."

"I wanted to get hold of you, tell you to be careful," she said. "I didn't know where you were. I finally tracked down Mason. He told me about Bill."

"I'm glad to know that you're okay," I said.

She reached out a hand. "What happened to your neck?"

"Nothing."

"Bullshit," she eyed the plump welt across my throat. "That's from a garrote."

"It's okay. It's almost healed."

She took off the sunglasses and those hazel eyes bore into me. "Someone tried for you, didn't they?"

I nodded. "Few nights ago."

"No I.D.?"

"Nothing."

"Did you call the police?"

"No."

Teri was going to say something else but changed her

mind. "Probably best." She got up and opened the cooler. "May I?"

"Help yourself."

She grabbed another beer and nodded at the papers. "What's that?"

"My big issue. Remember Bill's daughter, Tracy?"

She nodded. "The prodigal child."

"She's been arrested for murder." I gave her a quick outline. Teri listened without interruption. She was good at that. Sometimes she gave the impression that she wasn't listening but Teri missed little that went on around her. To some it was part of the training. For Teri, it came naturally.

"How did she know you were in town?"

"Well, I'm in the book," I said. "I do have a business to run."

"Don't you find it coincidental that she's been arrested while her father's been killed?"

"No," I said. "I don't find it coincidental. I think it's all related."

"But you don't know how?"

"No, I don't."

"But you're going to find out."

I lifted my beer in a toast. "You know me well."

"Yes," Teri smiled. "I do."

"So how did you find out about the others?"

"I still have a few connections at Langley," she said. "A girl friend of mine tipped me off, that there were whispers circulating in very small circles about the unit again."

She glanced into my eyes then quickly shifted her gaze back to the bay. "I started looking everyone up and found that many were dead."

"Did you call Bill?"

She nodded. "He already knew. Said that he was

working on it. Wouldn't tell me anything else. Said he didn't want to put me in danger."

"Has anyone...tried anything with you?"

"Not yet," Teri said. "But I felt a little vulnerable in L.A., especially with Gina and everything. Plus I wanted..." her voice trailed off.

"You were worried about me."

"Yeah, maybe a little," She downed the rest of her beer. "I want to see if there is a connection between everyone, maybe we can discover a pattern and find out who's behind it."

"So, you have the names?"

"And all the info on their deaths I've managed to un-cover."

"Do you have a place to stay?"

"As a matter of fact, I do. I rented a condo."

"What about your job in L.A.?"

"I took a leave of absence."

"Did you tell anyone where you were going? Boss, relatives, friends?"

"I told them I was going to Ohio to see family." Terry was from Iowa not Ohio. The lie was a good diversion in case it leaked to someone. She still wasn't looking at me. "I need your help with this, John."

I looked across the table. "That must have been hard for you to say."

"It was. Don't make me say it again. Besides, we can watch each other's backs."

"I'll make you a deal. You help me with Tracy's case, I help you."

"Quid pro quo, Clarice," Teri said in her best Hannibal Lecter voice.

"Except you're hotter than Jodie Foster," I said. We clinked our bottles together, sealing the deal.

TERI LEFT SOMETIME AROUND MID-AFTERNOON. An hour later, Jake Ross came on deck. The cop was dressed in jeans and a windbreaker and I saw the bulge of a weapon beneath it on his right hip.

He plopped down on the sofa. "Nice. I can't fault your view."

"It's home, Lieutenant. You appear off duty."

"That I am."

"Could I get you a beer?"

"I'd love one, thanks."

While I got the beer, Ross talked.

"I did my homework on you. John Anthony Logan, born in Michigan, raised in Japan. Black belts in Karate, Aikido, and Kenjutsu, and proficient in God knows how many other martial arts. Enlisted Special Forces, retired two years ago at rank of Major. You're clean with the state licensing board, too."

"I also like puppies and long walks in the moonlight."

"I heard you're working for Karen Lords."

"Someone's got to prove Tracy's innocence."

"You really think she's innocent?"

"Yes. How about you?"

He held up a hand. "Don't look at me, pal. We got taken off the case."

"What are you talking about?" I walked in and handed him the bottle. Ross took a big swallow.

"I mean Forsythe's body had barely made it to the M.E.'s

office before a black sedan pulls up and guys in dark suits get out."

"Feds?"

Ross nodded. "Just showed up as big as you please and took the whole show over. Kicked us out and charged the Rochelle girl with murder. My captain is not a happy man. He complained to the Commissioner, who did nothing."

"What gave the authority to horn in on a local murder investigation?"

"You know," Ross said. "I managed enough brain matter to ask them that very question. Said it was a federal matter and let it go at that. My boys are chomping at the bit."

"You think she's guilty?"

"I want to say yes," Ross said. "But my gut says no."

"Is it accurate?"

He paused. "Six months into Homicide my partner and I grab a case downtown. A businessman had been rolled in an alley. Wallet gone, a nice hole in his head. We canvassed and arrested a homeless guy who was wearing the businessman's jacket. He had the victim's blood on his hands. I watched him, I watched my partner interrogate him and he looked guilty as hell. Yet my gut said he didn't do it. He was homeless and a drunk but he couldn't have been a killer."

"So what did you do?"

"I dug some more. The murderer was the guy's business partner." He closed his eyes. "She didn't do it, Logan."

"I know."

"You're trying to find out the truth?"

"I am."

"Okay. I can't help you much but call me if you need something." He got up to leave.

"So what made you think the wino was innocent?"

He stopped and turned around. "Beats the hell out of

me. I just knew. He started to leave then swiveled again. "I think you're walking into a hornet's nest. Watch yourself."

"I always do."

"You should wear dress shirts and ties," Ross said and pointed to his neck. "It'll hide that better until it heals." He walked out before I could say anything.

8

James Forsythe owned, at last count, three homes in the US. His mansion in Coral Bay was located on a point of rock that overlooked the ocean and would have caused a bidding war in the real estate industry had he ever chose to sell it. The house was a three-story Colonial monstrosity with two wings branching off the main structure. There were purported to be three tennis courts and the largest private swimming pool in the state. The whole estate had been built from nothing, adhering to exacting specifications from Emily Forsythe and her husband. Any zoning or code problems were miraculously eliminated.

There was nothing to mark their driveway, no sign that said CAUTION: MILLIONAIRE AHEAD. Just a pair of wrought iron gates with a stylized F on them. They were tightly shut and monitored by a stern looking guard in a shed behind bulletproof glass. He came out, letting me see the .357 on his right hip. He took my name, checked a clipboard, asked for my ID and my PI license. Satisfied, he nodded and went back into the guard shack. The gates came open and I drove through. Maybe I should have washed my car.

The driveway was more like a private road. High palm trees bordered it in even spacing all the way to the house. The lawn looked so evenly cut that I got the notion that the groundskeeper actually measured each blade of grass. I pulled into the large circular driveway expecting a valet to step out and park my car but no one appeared so I made a guess as to a good spot and got out. I could hear the roar of the ocean but couldn't see it. Forsythe had planted thick trees and hedges to protect the ocean side of the home from paparazzi and the curious.

I stepped to the large double doors with another stylized F in relief on them and hit the doorbell. I heard the chimes of a Chopin piece. I wondered if he'd gotten that at the local hardware place.

The chimes had barely died when a stiff older man in an honest to goodness butler's waistcoat opened the door. He was tall and slim, with a face so slender it looked like it might slip off.

"You must be Mr. Logan." The accent was pure London. If you needed the typical English butler for a movie, this one would do nicely.

"That's correct."

"Mrs. Forsythe will see you in the family room. This way, please."

The foyer was as large as my boat. The floor was Spanish marble and so slick I was afraid I'd slip and break my neck. A framed painting of the Forsythe family hung on the wall. Forsythe looked dapper, his wife was smiling, and the kids looked stiff and bored. A winding stairway right out of Tara was to the right. I walked past immaculate formal living and dining rooms. I spotted a Gauguin and a

Van Gogh that didn't look like they were reprints. I felt sorry for the Forsythe kids. I wondered if they ever spilled a soft drink on the sofa, or let the dog loose in here. I didn't bet much on it. The place was as homey as a morgue.

To my relief, the butler led me to a large room that was more in tune with my tastes. The furnishings were nice but not too expensive. There was an LCD TV hanging above a stone fireplace. A small bar occupied the far corner with three stools and it was on one of them that a woman sat with her back to me.

"Mr. Logan, madam."

"Thank you, William." She turned and fixed an appraising glance at me with a pair of light green eyes.

If I had thought Emily Forsythe would be a disappointment in the looks department, I had been dead wrong. She would never see fifty again by all accounts but she didn't look it. The surgeries had been top notch, without the usual overt tightness and feature distortion that some women got with plastic surgery. Emily looked like a woman ten years younger. Her hair was a soft blond that fell around her face in large waves. She wore a one-piece peach blouse and shorts combination that wasn't the least bit loose and showed off every curve. The front was unzipped enough to show off the cleavage of enhanced breasts. The legs were long and toned. Her arms were tanned. Her only flaw, a small scar on her chin.

"Mr. Logan, so nice to meet you," she said and came off the stool with athletic ease. She took my hand. Her grip was firm.

"The pleasure is mine. Thank you for agreeing to see me."

She looked behind me. "See that we're not disturbed,

William." I heard the butler leave, shutting the door behind us.

Emily motioned me to a leather recliner. "Would you like a drink?"

"What do you have?"

"Anything you'd like."

I wanted something strong but professionalism won out. "Water is fine."

She went to the bar and picked up a highball glass. "Sorry. I started without you." She made me the drink, came over, bent down to hand it to me, and breasts covered my field of vision. She took her sweet time straightening back up.

"I'm very sorry about your husband," I managed to say.

"Thank you." She seemed to look at me for a moment, as though trying to read my mind. "I think perhaps you expected me to be dressed in black and mourning. Or even wailing, pouring my anger and hurt to God and the heavens?"

"It had occurred to me."

She smiled. "Well I've already done that this morning. Stayed in my room and had myself a good cry. Now it's time to move on."

"Doesn't sound very grief stricken to me."

"That's how Jim would have done it," she said. "I learned to do a lot of things being married to him." She took a large pull of her drink, held the glass up. "That's the first one I learned. Never drank so much as a beer until I met him."

"How nice."

"Let me tell you something about my husband, Mr. Logan. He could be the sweetest, gentlest man you'd ever meet. Then he could dress in his suit and go to the board room and destroy people's lives without as much as a second thought."

"I've known a lot of men like that."

"He was a rich, ego driven womanizer," she said, lifting her glass in a mock toast and staring heavenward. "Weren't you, darling?"

"Sounds like you don't care much that he's dead."

"Why lie to you, Mr. Logan? I could sit here and fake a cry and all that nonsense and you'd walk away saying how sad it all is. My respect for Jim died many years ago when I found out that he screwed our daughter's best friend."

"Divorce was an option."

"I thought about it," she said. "I've spent many nights alone in this house or two others that are just as big and just as empty as this one. I could have had it all. He would have divorced me and given me a nice settlement and I could have spent the rest of my life in luxury."

"So why didn't you?"

"Because I loved him. And believe it or not, he loved me in his own way."

"Most of us would have to take your word for it."

"Jim loved his company. That was his first true love and everything else in his life was behind it. Every person he ever slept with would soon be discarded like yesterday's newspaper. Except me. I was still here." She gave me another appraising glance. "So how did you end up a private detective?"

"Too many Raymond Chandler novels when I was a kid."

"Are you always so evasive?"

"I mean it. I read everything he ever wrote."

"You look like a dangerous man," she said. "I've heard you can be."

"Where did you hear that?"

"Another upside of being rich, Mr. Logan."

"I'm a teddy bear."

"You ever kill anyone?"

"I made someone upset once."

She smirked and took another pull of her drink.

"I'm here to ask you about the night of your husband's death."

"What would you like to know?" she asked. "Would you like a refill?"

I looked down at my empty glass. I hadn't realized I was drinking that fast. Perhaps it was the environment. "No thanks, Mrs. Forsythe, I'm fine."

"It's Emily," she said. "Sure?"

"Positive."

"I was here the night he was killed."

"Did he call you; tell you he was working late?"

"Jim didn't do that. He kept his schedule to himself most of the time. Of course I knew what a lot of it was and what he was doing." She seemed to think something over for a moment before she spoke. "Jim's latest flavor—this Rochelle girl. I understand you and her father are friends."

She didn't know about Bill's death. She referred to him in the present tense. Or was it deliberate? "You could say that. Do you know how they met?"

"She was...dancing at the Apollo. Jim went there and picked her up." She took another drink. "I may portray the loving stay at home wife, but I assure you I am not. I had Jim followed a lot, making sure of his whereabouts, who he was seeing, and trying to be proactive in heading off any scandals in the wake of his behaviors. When he picked up Ms. Rochelle in the Apollo that night, even my hired guy was surprised."

"Why is that?"

"He'd never gone there before. Not once in all these years. He went to strip clubs, Mr. Logan, lots of them, but always classy ones and exclusive private places in Miami."

"Must be hurtful seeing your husband with so many women."

She gave me another smile to cover up the daggers in her eyes. "It's amazing what you can get used to, isn't it?"

I guess it was. "Tracy has been charged for the murder."

"So why did you ask to see me?"

"I don't think she did it."

"Really?"

"She's confused and was under the influence the night he was killed. I don't think she was physically capable of killing him." I wanted to put the glass down but there wasn't a coaster and I was afraid of sitting it on anything.

"Sounds very tragic."

"I get the feeling you're not too angry with Tracy, Mrs. Forsythe—"

"—Emily," she corrected. "And no, I'm not. How could I be? You're stripping in a dive and a rich man offers you the world to go with him? Sure, she would do it. Lots of women would." She shifted her position on the bar stool, letting the full length of her legs play out. I had to force my eyes to stay on her face.

"Who would want to kill your husband, Emily?"

"Jim didn't get where he was without pulling a few noses out of joint. He had enemies on the city council and in Congress. He also had very powerful friends. So do I."

"I'm sure you do."

Emily Forsythe got up and walked over toward me. She wasn't completely steady on her feet but she did better than most people who'd downed two large highballs in the span of a few minutes. She sat down next to me and stretched those long legs out. "You're a very handsome man." Her words were beginning to slur.

"Thank you," I said. "But I think we should keep this strictly business, don't you?"

"Don't you think I'm attractive?"

"Yes."

"A man with principles. Let me tell you something about this day and age, Mr. Logan. No one would give a rat's ass if we did it or not. That's the best thing about being rich. I know, I've lived in that situation for years."

"You have to believe in something," I said.

"You know what I think? I think you may be the only guy in this town who really seems to care about who killed my husband."

"The authorities have pulled out all of their resources."

She giggled. She didn't seem like the giggly type. But she'd also had two highballs.

"Police. They're doing it because the city government tells them to. And the county politicians are worried about their coffers without Jim's big contributions. It's all a big dog and pony show."

I didn't know what to say to that. It seemed sad that a man died and his own wife didn't seem to care. Perhaps Forsythe had brought it upon himself but it still didn't seem right to me.

"Can you tell me anything about the deal with Micro-Corp?"

"Afraid not, handsome. I never dabbled in Jim's company. That was a no-no."

"Is there anyone I can see at the company who'd talk to me?"

"Perhaps I can arrange something." Her voice purred.

The zipper on her jumpsuit had moved south another inch or two.

"I'd appreciate that, Mrs. Forsythe."

"Emily," she said again.

"Emily."

She licked her lips with the tip of a pink tongue. "So you think the murderer is connected to the Company?"

"I'm not thinking anything. I'm asking and probing and seeing what surfaces."

"Probing," she said. A lecherous smile found its way to her mouth. "An interesting term."

"Know any business associate of your husband's named Frank?"

"No, sorry." She inched closer and ran a finger along my jaw. "God, you're a handsome bastard."

I got up and handed her my card. "I'd appreciate a phone call if you think of anything."

She pouted. "Spoil sport."

I got up. "Thanks for the drink."

9

Teri and I flew to D.C. saying little to each other on the flight. We were lost in our memories of Bill and Teri knew it was especially painful for me so she didn't push. Just left me to my thoughts. At one point, she reached over and squeezed my hand and that was all that was said.

The funeral procession left Washington National Cathedral, crossed over the Potomac, and traveled down to the nation's most famous resting place. Politicians, CEO's and friends spanning decades attended the service for Major General William Rochelle. Tracy would not be here. Her lack of a permanent residence, her drug habits, and general lack of regard for boundaries, all combined to deem her a flight risk by a judge. Bail was denied despite Karen's best efforts.

I hadn't been to Arlington National Cemetery in years but I'd never forgotten the silent majesty of the place. Rows of white marble stones spoke of heroes and honor, of battles fought and won and lost. The original section of the cemetery had been created in what had once been Mrs. Robert E. Lee's rose garden. The General and his family had long since left Arlington, displaced by the war that had torn the nation apart, and moved further south. The story holds that Lincoln's quartermaster had suggested putting a cemetery there so that if Lee ever returned he could not look out the window without seeing what he had done.

Sweat ran down my back, soaked my shirt, and made my clothes stick to me. I watched from a distance, not wanting to advertise my presence. The priest droned on, saying words that seemed meaningless in the humidity.

Teri stood next to me in a black dress. I knew she was scanning the crowd the same as I was, looking for faces that didn't belong. Murderers like to show up at their victim's funerals. No one's really paying attention to you; they're all busy grieving over the dearly departed or catching up with someone they haven't seen in decades. They can blend into the background and no one notices.

It's also a good place for an assassin to scope out his next target.

"Anything?" Teri whispered.

"Zip," I answered. There were CEO's, members of the Joint Chiefs of Staff, the Directors of the FBI, CIA, and members of the NSA among the crowd. They stood lost in thought, gazing quietly as the flag was folded. The honor guard brought rifles to shoulders.

"Ready...? Fire..."

Shots rolled across the peaceful landscape. I felt Teri twitch at the first volley. Gunfire was gunfire, no matter where you were.

The final words were said and it was done. I waited until the gravesite was barren of people. I went up, oblivious to any curious stares, and stopped before the coffin that held the mortal remains of my boss, my friend, my mentor, and my surrogate father. There would be no talk. Any secrets Bill wished to impart on me were gone forever. They died with him with the crack of a sniper's rifle.

I brought my arm up in a slow salute, tip of middle finger touching the right brow, held it, then slowly eased it down. There was nothing more to say. I turned and Teri joined me on the walk back to the car.

"Major Logan!"

A fellow in a Brooks Brother's suit with the posture of a bodyguard approached me, his brown hair in a crew cut similar to Killian.

"Senator Hardaway would like to drive you back to your hotel."

"Tell the Senator thanks, but I have a ride."

"I'm afraid he insists," the man said. I heard Teri exhale slightly, a habit she had when she prepared for trouble. I reached over and squeezed her hand.

"Since you put it that way." I turned to her. "I'll see you back at the hotel."

She didn't want to but she nodded and turned toward the car. I caught her watching as the bodyguard led me to the stretch limo, opened the door, and followed me inside.

Senator Franklin Hardaway hadn't changed much in the years since I'd seen him. He was a large, bulldog-faced man who had been born into a poor southern family. He had worked his tail off to get an education then turned to politics. He had a reputation of possessing a classic political savvy even in the days when I was in the DC circles. While most Americans couldn't name more than a handful of Senators, Hardaway had made his name known during the Gulf War. CNN had shown him in desert fatigues, standing with the troops in the Saudi desert. With his huge face in the camera, he'd issued a challenge to Saddam to come out and "settle this thing man to man." He'd won his next reelection by a landslide and the public loved him. I knew him to have the tenacity to go toe to toe with the biggest political opponents on the Hill. Most of the time he won.

His bodyguard sat across from me in the limo. The door closed and the outside world disappeared. He made a motion and I opened my jacket, showing him I had no weapon.

"That won't be necessary, Ray."

Hardaway sat to Ray's left. The Senator wore a black tailored suit and a large diamond clasp in his black tie. Ray nodded and opened a section between the seats to my right and slipped out. The partition closed and we were alone again.

"Cute," I said. "Do you have a little wheel for him to play on?"

"Ray doesn't know you like I do," Hardaway said. "You could kill him or me without a gun, isn't that right? All of Rochelle's people could." He lifted the vodka tonic in his hand. "Drink?"

"No, thanks."

"Suit yourself," he said.

"Now that the pleasantries are over, Senator, what can I do for you?"

"Let's talk about the late Major General William Rochelle."

"So talk."

Hardaway ran his tongue over his front teeth. "I hear his daughter is in some trouble."

"You heard correctly."

"A shame, that girl," Hardaway said. "Very smart, but prefers heroin to Hemingway from what I hear. Anyway, what's your interest in all of this?"

"In all of what?"

Hardaway chuckled. "You're working to clear her name, aren't you?"

"Whether I am or not is really none of your business, I think."

"That's the problem," Hardaway said. "You think wrong. James Forsythe had a proposal to buy MicroCorp on the table. You ever hear about that?"

"They tell me it's front page news, Senator."

"Rich people make powerful enemies, Logan. Forsythe had them here in the Beltway, believe me."

"That's why I don't think the girl killed him."

"You might be right," Hardaway said. "But I'm going to give you a piece of advice. Let it go."

"And why would I want to do that?"

He took a sip and heaved a sigh of approval. "Because I want you to come work for me."

I laughed. "You're kidding me."

"I'm as serious as a crutch, Major. Between you and me, I have my eye on the White House in three years. You come on board and you can ride the train with me."

"Senator, you're forgetting that you spent a lot of time trying to get Bill Rochelle fired, court-martialed, or both. Now you want me to work for you?"

Hardaway's jowls flapped as he shook his head. "That was all politics, son. It never happened, did it? Because I had no intentions of doing such a thing. I admired the hell out of your boss. Medal of Honor winner and all that—hell, he was a poster boy for Uncle Sam. And you—" He gestured at me. "—you're as good. Ribbons, citations, and years of service. Come work for me and I'll give you an office and you won't have much to do when you show up. You can spend a lot of time "on special assignments" for me. And women...Logan, D.C. is crawling with women who love to screw guys in powerful offices."

"And what would I be doing?"

"You could advise me on military matters. I have a couple of big bills coming to the floor soon. You could help me make sense of it."

"Thanks for the offer, Senator, but I think I'll pass."

Hardaway held up his hands. "Logan, I'm a good judge of people and I know that Rochelle recruited the best. I know you. You're better than what's become of you. Living on a rickety houseboat and eking out a living as a private dick in Florida? Are you kidding me?"

"It's my life, Senator," I said. "I can look at my face in the mirror."

"Conscience is overrated, especially in this town," Hardaway said. "Name your salary, Logan. I'll get it for you."

"I've got a client back home. It would be bad for business if I cut and run."

"The Rochelle girl is trouble," Hardaway said. "She's a dope head, a boozer, and from what I hear, she'll screw anything on two legs, man or woman." He shook his head. "Hard to believe she's her father's daughter."

"Everyone has a right to justice, Senator."

"I can see that she gets a slap on the wrist," Hardaway said. "Jail would be the best place for her, really. She'd sober up and get clean."

"Who do you think killed him?"

A chuckle. "Who the hell knows? Forsythe had a Japanese company competing with him over MicroCorp. He was killed with one of those nip swords. Maybe they did it." He finished his drink, his face flushed.

"Come on board, Logan. I can use a man of your talents."

"To do what? Give your image a boost with the veterans and advise you whether or not to vote for a missile system or a new rifle for the troops?"

Hardaway smiled. "How about Ambassador to Japan?"

I froze.

"I know all about you. Growing up in Japan, you know the culture, their strengths, and their weaknesses. You know when they lie and how they lie and how to penetrate their lies. I want a new trade agreement with them when I'm elected. You could help me get that."

"I'm not a bureaucrat, Senator. I'm just an old soldier living a quiet life."

"Dammit, boy, you're making a mistake."

"I've made them before," I said. The limo pulled to a halt. "I think this is my stop. Thanks for the offer, Senator, but no thanks."

His eyes bored into my back as I got out. Teri waited for me in the hotel lobby. She was out of the funeral attire and had changed into jeans and a tee shirt. I hadn't realized the ride had taken that long.

"What happened?"

"Hardaway wants me to forget Tracy and work for him. If he's elected President, I'll be Ambassador to Japan."

"Why would he offer you such a thing?"

I shrugged. "Why would he?"

"Especially when he hated Bill's guts," Teri said.

I nodded. "There are a lot of questions to be answered."

David Chang met me at a small restaurant just off Pennsylvania Avenue. David was of both Chinese and Japanese heritage and was one of the best spies in the business. I knew it because I had recruited him from MIT and trained him. He now ran the unit that Bill Rochelle once commanded, although I'd heard the mission of the unit had changed with the more politically correct times.

"Good to see you, John," David shook my hand. He wore a tan sport jacket and gray slacks and his shoes were buffed to a nice sheen. "You look well."

"So do you."

We sat. I ordered a Crown and Coke. David ordered a gin and tonic.

"It was a nice service," he said.

"It was."

"I noticed that Tracy wasn't there. I'm assuming she was denied bail."

I nodded. "So you heard about her little trouble."

"More than little, wouldn't you say?"

I guess I would. Our drinks came and we savored the first tastes before I spoke. "David, I need your help."

"Sure."

"What do you know about Bill's death?"

"Sniper. Sneaked onto the estate and shot him through the sliding glass doors. I offered my help off the record but as you know I have to keep it low key. I do have the covert nature of the unit to think of."

"Did you look into it, David?"

"Of course I did. You weren't the only one who loved that old man."

"Find out anything?"

"Nothing. No prints, no leads. It could have been anyone. Checked the house for bugs, checked his schedule, everything. I'm checking passenger photos from all the airports and train stations for the past two weeks but you know how successful that will be." David shook his head. "Damndest thing."

"How goes the job?"

"Not like the old days. More politics and paper pushing. Langley keeps on my ass. I think...we might be getting phased out come budget time."

"You're kidding."

"Without Bill's influence," he shook his head. "I don't know if I can keep the wheels going or not."

"You'll figure it out," I said. "You were always much savvier about those things than I ever was."

"You taught me a lot, John."

"You were my best," I said. "And I'm proud of you."

"Are you keeping out of trouble?"

"Trying to."

David laughed. "You always did wreak havoc." His face turned serious. "I shouldn't tell you this, but there is a club in Miami. You know of it?"

"Carl's place?"

David nodded, just a slight movement of his head. "He's still there. You might pay him a visit."

"He won't see me."

Chang smiled. "You'll think of something."

"Can you let me know if anything important turns up?"

"Sure will. I'm sorry I don't have more for you."

I nodded. "It's okay."

"I saw Teri with you. She looks good."

"Yeah, she does."

"Things back together with you two?"

I shrugged. "We'll see."

"One more thing, John."

"Yeah?"

"They may have forgiven you for your little stunt but

they've not forgotten. You're *persona non grata* in places around here."

"I know."

David gave me a slight smile. "Just thought I'd re-mind you."

10

That night, Teri and I took the late flight home. Teri had wanted to go to Bill's house but I wasn't up for it. There were too many memories in the place. Any idea I had to try to look there for clues would be a wasted effort. At this point, I had no idea what I would even be looking for, anyway.

Instead, I went to jail. I had a few more questions.

Tracy walked into the room. She was pale but her eyes were sharper. She sat down across the partition from me and picked up the phone.

"Hey, kid."

She managed a smile. "Hey, samurai."

"Are you hanging in there?"

"Yeah," she said. "It's been rough, especially the detox. I didn't think I was hooked, but..."

"You're gonna beat this, Tracy."

"What about the other?"

"I'm still working on it," I said. "I think all of this may have something to do with your father."

She snorted. "Big surprise there."

"Tracy, do you know if Jim knew your dad?"

"Yeah, they did."

I almost jumped off my seat. "How?"

"I don't know. Jim told me that they knew each other. I asked him but he wouldn't explain."

"Did he tell you anything else?"

"He told me that he was doing my dad a favor and it was gonna reap good benefits later on for him."

"Did he say what it was?"

"No. When I asked him, he said 'it's nothing you need to get involved in'."

"Did he tell you anything about his deal with Micro-Corp?"

"No. But he did say that he was having a problem getting something through Congress and needed a break."

"Okay," I said. "You hang in there. We're gonna get this resolved."

She smiled. Her hand shook. She reached out and brought palm to glass. I did the same, our hands together yet apart.

"I'm sorry, samurai. I've been an idiot."

"It's all in the past, Tracy. Use the time in here to get clean and sober and think about what you want to do. I'm gonna get you out."

"How was the...you know?"

"It was nice. They buried him with full honors and a lot of important people showed up."

"Wish I could have been there." Tears filled her eyes. "Dammit..."

I didn't know what to do so I simply let her cry.

"It hurts so much..."

"Pain does that. But it will ease."

"What could you know about pain?"

"More than you know," I answered.

KAREN LORDS and I met for dinner so we could compare notes. Karen bought. I guess a lawyer could afford it.

"Forsythe's deal with MicroCorp had to go through the Senate Foreign Trade Committee," Karen said. "Without their support he didn't have a snowball's chance of getting it."

I picked up my knife and cut the sirloin in front of me. "So, who's on the Committee?"

Karen picked up her cell. "I can find out." She pressed a button and moment later said, "Dinah? I need you to go online. I need the names of all the senators who are on the Senate Foreign Trade Committee and call me when you have it." She clicked off. "Dinah's my assistant. She can find anything."

"Was that the attractive woman who gave me water the other day in your office?"

"It was."

"Nice to have good help."

"That's what's keeping you small-time," she said. "You need some assistants."

"Can't afford them. I can barely afford me."

Karen had a glass of merlot and she took a sip. "Why do you do this? I've read some of your background. A man with your experience could be making a lot of money in Miami. There are two security firms down there who would pay you a ton for your expertise."

"I do a little consulting work," I said. "But I've spent most of my life working for other people, having to do what they said and go where I was told. Now I work for me. I decide what cases I'll take and how to work them. I make a decent living and I have a couple of investments. My late wife's father was a banker and he set us up with a nice portfolio. I may not be rich but I'm doing okay."

"I'm sorry about her."

"Thanks."

"How about the police force?"

"I thought about it but decided I'd be working for someone else. I prefer this. When my wife died it was my work that kept me sane."

"You got someone special now?"

"Not really." I wondered if the question was leading somewhere. "You?"

"No one special."

"How'd you get into law?"

"I wanted to be a dancer. Took lessons from the time I was five. Tap, ballet, modern, I wanted to be a star."

"So what happened?"

"I wasn't good enough," she said. "It took me a decade just to admit that to myself. I was good and I had some talent, but not enough to get me there. I ended up in college and chose law because I could make good money they said. Turns out I was a natural."

"I can't argue with that." Her cell phone rang. "Thank you," was all she said before snapping it shut. She looked at me. "The Senate Foreign Trade Committee is chaired by its senior member, Franklin Hardaway."

"That's interesting."

"How so?"

I told her about being in D.C. for Bill's funeral and meeting with Hardaway. "He wanted me to stop snooping and to let the feds handle it."

"Why would he care?"

"Why indeed?"

"Curious." She checked her watch and finished her vodka tonic. "I need to go, Mr. Logan."

The abruptness wasn't lost on me. "Okay. Thanks for dinner."

WILLIAM LED me over the flagstone walkway lined with tall hibiscus forming a natural privacy fence around the enormous pool. It looked to be three times the size of an Olympic one. Emily Forsythe was half way across, her strokes smooth and efficient.

William motioned me to a table and chairs beneath a red striped umbrella.

"Can I get you anything, sir?"

"I'm fine, thank you."

William gave a discreet glance at the pool before walking away.

Emily finished the lap and turned back, kicking off the wall and gliding out a quarter of the distance before resuming her crawl. There was very little splash.

She ended at the wall nearest to me. Her head popped up and she pushed wet hair from her face.

"Hello," I said.

She smiled. "I wasn't expecting you so soon."

"As I said on the phone, I'd be right over."

"So you did." She moved to the ladder and climbed out. She was naked as the day she was born. Her body was toned and tanned. She walked over without a bit of concern where a blue towel lay folded on the table beside me. "See? If I'd known you were coming, I'd have put something on."

"Sorry. Does William mind you prancing around in nothing?"

"No. He's seen it all before. He's third generation butler. He knows better than to ogle the boss. And I know better than to sleep with the help." She dried off and took her sweet time about it. I was tempted to avert my gaze but I didn't. She was trying to get a reaction from me. I stared but with indifference, as though looking at a painting.

"You like what you see?"

"Sure," I said. "Any man would."

"Except my husband," she said. "He was after the younger ones." She wrapped the towel around her. "You stared at least."

"You flaunt it, honey, I'm gonna look."

She smiled. "So to what do I owe this visit?"

"Tell me about your husband and Bill Rochelle."

"I told you he didn't know your friend."

"And you were wrong. Or you were lying."

She pursed her lips. "When I spoke to you the other day I wasn't aware of Jim's association with Mr. Rochelle. Since then, I have uncovered facts to the contrary."

"Like what?"

"Jim made some phone calls to Baltimore. I had the number checked. It was Mr. Rochelle's number."

"How many calls?"

"Ten in all."

William magically appeared with a pitcher of iced tea and two glasses. He poured a glass for Emily and then me when I gave him the nod.

"Lemon?" he asked.

"Sure, but be careful. I could get spoiled."

"Certainly, sir," he said, slipping a slice of fresh lemon on the rim of my glass.

When he left, I said, "So when did the calls start?"

"First one was about two years ago. The last one was a little over five weeks ago."

"You looked back that far?"

"Of course not. That's why I hire men like you."

"Any idea what the calls were about?"

She sipped her tea. "No idea. Jim kept his business pretty close to the vest."

"Anything you could find out would be a help."

"I'll see what I can do," she said. "You really are serious about finding Jim's killer?"

"Yes," I nodded. "Because if I don't an innocent girl goes to jail."

"You're a softy, Mr. Logan."

"Don't tell anyone," I said. "I have a reputation to protect."

"Promise."

I drank the tea and stared at the pool. "What else did you not tell me?"

"Nothing."

"Suit yourself. But it's your husband that ended up with a samurai sword run through him. If Tracy didn't do it then the killer is still out there. Maybe his reason for killing your husband wasn't business but personal. Maybe he might try you next."

"Now you're just trying to frighten me."

"Hopefully you're right," I shrugged. "But I'd hire a few extra security people just in case."

"I'll help you, Mr. Logan. Any way that I can."

I got up. "Thanks for the tea. And the view."

"Glad you enjoyed them." She uncrossed her legs and the towel wasn't long enough.

"Both of them," I said. I tore my eyes away and walked

out. I felt like the geek in high school who'd just met the prettiest cheerleader in school. I turned back and she'd dropped the towel. She gave me another view before she waved and dived back into the pool.

William escorted me out.

"She's something else," I said. "Must be difficult working around someone who's naked all the time."

"You get so you don't notice it," William said. "She's just lonely, Mr. Logan. She has a good heart. You should see her when she's on one of her charity missions to Haiti, holding those kids. She comes home and weeps for days over them."

"Doesn't act like a widow."

"The marriage was in name only," William said. "They liked each other but she'd lost all respect and trust for him."

"Anything you can tell me about your boss and why someone might kill him?"

"He had his faults," William said. "He always treated me fair and paid me well." He shook his head. "I'm afraid I don't have any idea who'd want him dead."

"What about General Rochelle? Ever see him around?"

"No, sir, can't say as I ever did." He opened my car door. "There you go, sir. Drive safely."

He shut it and I watched him walk back into the house.

Ten minutes into the drive home, I realized someone was following me.

11

IT WAS A CREAM-COLORED SEDAN WITH A HEAVY FRAME AND A lot of horses under the hood. I spotted it lagging two cars behind me. I changed lanes and took the next exit to see if it followed me. It did. I took another couple of turns. For a moment, it didn't appear to have made the last turn and I almost let out a sigh of relief. Then it rounded the corner and headed toward me.

I had a few options. I could confront them in the middle of the street. Just stop the car, get out, and say 'what do you want' or something John Wayne-ish like that. If there were more than one of them—and I was betting there would be —I'd be outmanned and outgunned. I'd fight bravely, worthy of song and epic poem, but I'd still be dead.

I could try to lose them with a Hollywood style car chase through the streets of Coral Beach, but he had horsepower and, for all I knew, another tail car somewhere. If he cut me off in some secluded street, I'd be in a firefight.

The third option suited me better. I drove at a leisurely pace through the winding streets and back onto Ocean Boulevard. Six blocks later the sedan was still on me as I pulled into the parking lot of the new Beach Center Mall. Two stories of American consumerism at its finest. I parked and headed toward the main entrance, keeping an eye on the car.

This posed a problem for the sedan folks. If they wanted to tail me, they would have to get out and follow me inside. That strategy exposed them, made them more vulnerable. If they had orders to maintain loose surveillance, they could simply wait in the parking lot and keep an eye on my car until I reappeared. Until they made a move, I wouldn't know how serious they were.

I disappeared amid the throngs of shoppers entering the mall and watched what they did. The car pulled up to the entrance and two medium built men in dark suits got out. The car sped back into the parking lot.

They weren't stupid. I would have done the same thing. Two men to tail the target—me—and the driver could watch the parking lot in case I lost the tails and doubled back to my car.

I dialed Teri. She answered on the second ring. "What's up?"

"I need your help," I said. "I need you to come to the Beach Center Mall. I've got two goons following me and one in the parking lot babysitting my car."

"Want to give them the slip?"

"That's the general idea."

"So what's the plan?"

"Pull on the west side of the mall and stay handy. I'll phone you when I'm ready to come out."

"Be there in thirty," she said.

I used the shop windows to monitor them. A true pro would know by my actions that I was aware of them, but they seemed oblivious. They strolled along, acting as if they were blending in with the crowd but standing out like a neon sign. I went to the food court on the second floor and got a slice of pizza and a soda. I sat down in a corner spot where I could see the whole court. That threw them a little; they lounged on a bench just outside the court across from a Gap. An artificial palm tree partially obstructed their view.

The hallway to the restrooms was to the right of my table. I finished the food and waited until their eyes weren't on me, then I slipped down the hall and into the men's room. Only a younger man with a small boy was inside. The man was helping the boy wash his hands. I went into a stall and waited. A moment later the man and boy left and all was quiet.

They'd look up and see I was gone. They'd spend a few frantic seconds looking for me. Either way, they'd have to assume that I'd gone to the bathrooms. They'd have to check.

Blood pounded in my ears. My Glock rested easily against my hip but I didn't want gunfire. The last thing I needed was mall security chasing me through a hundred potential witnesses. I glanced at my watch. Teri should be pulling in any minute. My breath quickened, the body taking in more oxygen in preparation for combat. Who were they? FBI, NSA? Were they there to simply monitor me or kill me? My hand instinctively found the fading welt on my neck.

The bathroom door opened. I let out a nice sigh, flushed the toilet, and came out of the stall. Bathrooms were great if you needed to kick someone's ass. There were lots of hard surfaces.

Only one had come in. He stood at the sink, absently washing his hands. I walked up beside him and washed mine, glancing his way.

"Hey," I said.

He nodded.

I dried my hands and turned to leave. I felt him move toward me and heard the click of a knife. I dropped my right shoulder and moved left. My arm came around to trap his left arm, my right hand on his left shoulder blade to push him face-first into the wall. He bounced, the knife clattered from his hands, and he turned toward me. Blood poured from his nose. He tried a karate kick. I blocked it and kicked him in the knee. He started to go down and I grabbed the back of his head and slammed his face into the sink. He slumped to the floor.

The door opened and his friend was there, apparently thinking his partner was taking too long, hence there was a problem. He took the scene in a glance and reached beneath his arm. I spotted the outline of a pistol there. I dropped, kicking the back of his knee. His leg buckled and he went down, still clawing for the pistol. I smashed a forearm into his face, and then introduced his nose to my knee. He collapsed with a groan.

I walked down the hallway and back into the court. I called Teri.

"Where are you?" She asked.

"Me and the dynamic duo had a bit of a tussle in the men's room," I said. "Just like grade school."

"You all right?" Was that concern in her tone?

"Fine. I'm hitting the door in ten seconds."

She pulled up in a silver colored Sunfire just as I came out. I got into the car and she took off through the parking lot.

"Drive around toward my car," I said. "I want to see what the remaining member or members are doing."

"You think he'll go in?"

"We'll see."

"Who were they?"

"Didn't get a chance to check for I.D.," I said. "I wanted to get out of there. But the one guy sported a nice Emerson CQ combat knife. Looks like his partner had a compact Beretta with custom grips. I didn't get a chance to get a closer look."

"No?"

"He was trying to pull it on me at the time."

Teri smiled and weaved the car expertly through the lot. I showed her where the sedan was and she parked a discreet distance. She reached behind the seat and brought up a pair of small binoculars.

"One guy behind the wheel," she said. "He looks worried."

"I don't want to get you involved in this, Teri."

"Too late. I'm already involved."

"I mean, this is my fight—"

"No, John," she said, still watching the car. "This is our fight. It's our fight because someone tried to kill you and have managed to kill our old teammates. Bill's dead and Gina's dead, along with a dozen others. Don't tell me it's not my fight."

I sighed.

"Wait, he's getting out," Teri said.

The driver walked quickly into the mall.

"Checking on his teammates?"

"They had micro receivers in their ears," I said. "Probably told him they were down. I got one of their knees pretty good."

"You still practice karate?"

"Yes."

"Nice." She smiled. "We'll have to spar soon. Go get your

car, the coast is clear."

They'd come out not only to find they'd lost me, but that I'd managed to double back and take my car from beneath their noses.

Score: Logan two, inadequate surveillance crew nothing.

東

I TOOK extra precautions going back to the houseboat. Satisfied that I wasn't being followed, I stepped on board and made myself a sandwich and beer. A half hour later, Teri came on board with Killian.

"I followed the motley crew to a Days Inn on the beach," Teri said. "They weren't too happy."

"Did you get a room number?"

Teri rolled her eyes. "Of course."

"Then I'll have to pay them a visit soon," I said. I turned to Killian, who was grabbing two beers from the fridge. "Any news on your end?"

"Well, if Amber, the mysterious call girl, is local, only one guy in town would know," Killian said. "And I've arranged a meeting with him for you."

"And who might that be?"

"His name is Derby Puckett. He runs a high-class bordello out of his home in West Cove."

Teri said, "You're kidding."

"Tom Clancy couldn't make it up," Killian said. "Been there for years."

"And he's agreed to see me."

"With me tagging along, of course. I do work for him from time to time."

"What kind of work?" Teri said.

"Charming the ladies," Killian said. He handed her one of the beers.

"Still your usual smartass self, Mason," Teri shook her head. "Some things never change."

"Now that you two are reacquainted," I said. "What can we deduce about the guys in the mall?"

"Feds," Teri said. "Not FBI. I don't think NSA, either."

"No clue from their license plate?"

Teri shook her head. "Rental car. Pretty sanitized. Could be anybody."

"I know someone who might have some info in Miami," I said. "I'll get down there and see him. Teri, you can accompany me for that. You might come in handy."

She nodded. "Nice to know I'm good for something."

Killian looked at his watch. "We need to go if we're going to see Derby."

"Can I have another beer while you're gone?" Teri asked, looking over at me.

"As long as you replenish the stock with equal quality stuff."

She made a mock pout. "I thought you might say that."

I checked my Glock and stuck it in my holster. Killian and I went out. It was late afternoon, the evening rush hour looming on the horizon. The city seemed to be gearing up for it as a boxer in the dressing room prepares for the fight with just minutes away.

Killian gave me little glances of his head as he drove.

"What?"

"Nothing," he said. "None of my business."

"Teri?"

He gave one of those Killian shrugs, barely any movement.

"You don't want her help?"

"Didn't say that."

"She's good, Kil. She's proven herself more than once while she was on my team. She's sharp."

"No argument there. It's not about her skills in the field."

"Then what?"

He sighed. "About you and her."

"That was a long time ago."

"Women can mess up your thinking."

"I'm fine. It's not like we're hopping back in the sack."

"It's a matter of time, bro."

"And if it does?"

"Someone has a contract on your old unit, bro. I saw you when Shikira died. I don't want to see you like that again. You get involved with Teri and something happens to her, you're going to either crawl into a bottle again or seek revenge. You won't be thinking straight when you do it and you'll wind up dead." Killian hit the exit ramp. "There. I said my peace."

"You're a secret sentimentalist."

"Damned Irish in me," Killian said.

12

DERBY PUCKETT WAS A TOWERING HULK OF A BLACK MAN WITH a baldhead and an ugly scowl that made him look like the gangster in *Pulp Fiction*. His home was a nondescript ranch house on the beach and we sat on the patio by the pool watching the waves breaking on the shore. Three girls in the briefest of swimwear frolicked in the pool. They looked barely out of high school.

"Killian here says you're cool." Derby said in a deep bass.

"He told you that I needed some information."

Derby nodded. "About a girl named Amber."

"That's right."

"Forsythe was a regular customer of mine. Took good care of the girls, never beat 'em or anything. He paid well. One night he calls me. Says he's entertaining a special guest and he needs a special girl. Didn't want one of the locals, wanted an out of town one."

"Did he say why?"

"Just that it was what he wanted."

"So what did you do?"

"I called up a fellow associate of mine in Miami. I

arranged for the girl matching his specifications to come up. Forsythe paid her travel expenses through me. Cash."

"No tracks," I said.

"Such is the way of this business. Lots of cash, no paper trails."

"I need to talk to this girl."

"My friend won't like you nosing around," Derby said. "He's not as nice as I am."

"Can you arrange it?"

"What's in it for me?"

"The girl may be a witness to a murder. Eventually, the feds might come nosing in your or your friend's operation. The sooner I can get to her, the less likely the feds won't. With me you get nice and discreet."

Derby turned to Killian. "Is he discreet?"

"I couldn't even find out how much."

Derby snorted. "Watch that smart mouth, Killian."

Killian said, "Careful, I'm getting shaky."

There was a moment of tension in the air. Derby sighed. "All right, I'll see what I can do."

"I appreciate it." We both got up and shook hands.

"I let Killian here know when I get something."

"Perfect."

I walked off the patio and toward the car but I wasn't so far away that I couldn't hear what Killian said to Derby.

"I owe Logan my life a couple of times over. You try to screw him and all bets are off. I'll kill you and burn your fancy whorehouse to the ground."

"So where are we on this thing?"

"I'm working on finding this Amber girl. I have a feeling

she operates out of Miami. I've got some people tracking her down." I sipped some water. "How's the client?"

"She's holding on by her teeth," Karen said. "She's spent a lifetime stuffing her body full of anything and everything."

"A shame. She's actually a bright girl."

"Some women believe their only assets lie in their looks," Karen said. "Tracy traded her brain power for her ability to seduce guys in return for getting whatever she wanted." She scribbled something down on a note pad and put the pen down hard. "The whole damn city's ready to railroad this girl. She may not be Mother Teresa but she didn't kill her sugar daddy."

I sat the water down. "There is a connection between Forsythe and Tracy's father."

"What is it?"

"That's just it. I don't know. Tracy told me they knew each other but didn't know how."

"If we can find that connection, our questions may be answered." Karen straightened her desk as she talked. "How do we do that?"

"I have an old acquaintance in Miami who might know. I'm headed down there."

"Are you asking me for expense money?"

"It'll be on my bill."

"Thanks."

I stood by the window gazing out at the city. It looked different from up here. Cleaner. Prettier. The Bay seemed bluer, the bridge shinier. Karen moved beside me.

"It looks so calm, so tranquil, doesn't it?"

"Yes."

"Hard to believe it's filled with so many asses," she said. "Are you hungry?"

"Is that an invite to dinner?"

"Sure. I'm getting too maudlin to stay in the office. Much more of this and I'll be ready to throw myself on the mercy of the court." She turned. "Let's go."

I followed her to a two-story house overlooking the beach. I was all too aware of the implications, as well as the risk of breaking a professional relationship. The dangers were in the back of my head, sounding like alarm bells. I let them ring as she unlocked the door and I followed her inside. Soft hues of greens and blues deco-rated the walls. A bookcase held an assortment of volumes, old and new. There were books ranging from Bartlett's Quotations to the latest thrillers to Moby Dick.

Karen noticed me. "A good quotation comes in handy in closing arguments sometimes." She took off her coat and offered to take mine before disappearing down the hall.

"This is nice."

"Spoils from the divorce," she called out from down the hall.

She appeared a minute later, now in jeans and a tee shirt. She got me a beer and a glass of wine for her and began to pull things from the fridge. In no time, she was at the counter chopping furiously. I went beside her. "Anything I can do?"

"Can you chop something without losing your finger?"

"Of course."

She handed me a tomato. "Chop that for a salad."

I grabbed a knife and made quick work of it, tossing it in the bowl.

"Impressive."

"What, the men in your life don't cook?"

She laughed. "There hasn't been a man in my life for a while."

"Career first?"

"Yes, unfortunately. My ex husband also chose the same philosophy. We both knew it going in and told ourselves that we could make it work. We couldn't."

I was aware of how close our bodies were. "What did he do?"

"He was in corporate law."

Dinner didn't take long to prepare and we ate mostly in silence, each of us lost in our own thoughts. I knew what was about to happen and so did she. Problem was, I also knew that no woman could have that part of me yet. Maybe never.

The meal had ended with small talk. We spoke of careers, life, and music, of philosophy, poetry, and current events. Karen asked about the work of a P.I. When the conversation began to drag she went into the kitchen to do dishes.

I followed her. "You didn't invite me here just for dinner, did you?"

Her eyes closed and she sighed. "This is breaking every rule in my book, Logan."

"I know," I said. My arms circled her waist. She felt good. Warm and tender in my embrace.

I stepped back. "I'm sorry. I can't."

She turned around to face me. I already saw the question.

"You are a beautiful woman. She's only been dead a year."

"And you don't know where you stand with it."

"Yeah."

"I'm sorry," she said. "I didn't mean to get my signals crossed."

"You didn't. I came here knowing what you were wanting

and I was hoping that I could. But I can't. Not yet." I hugged her and kissed her on the cheek.

"I need to go."

She didn't say anything as I let myself out.

THE DRIVE HOME was complicated by troubling thoughts. Thoughts of women. First Karen and the obvious attraction we both felt for each other. Then they drifted on to Teri.

Seeing her again after all of this time had bothered me in ways I didn't expect. Once, in another lifetime, she and I were two spies caught up in the certainty of our duties to Uncle Sam and positive of God's divine blessings upon each life we took, each enemy of America that we destroyed. Our relationship had been marred by contradictions. Passion was tempered by the defense of the covert operative: emotional detachment, that wall that enables you to kill other human beings without ending up a casualty of your own conscience. It enabled you to lie, scheme, and dive into the foul sewers of human existence without contaminating your own soul. We let it go on longer than we should have and both walked away battered and scarred from it.

With Teri back in my life, even for a brief time, the scars had resurfaced and I felt a desire for something that could never be. We were older, more mature, and I knew that emotionally, I would be incapable of giving any woman my heart. Shikira had been my soul mate, a once in a lifetime love that most men never find. A year after her ashes were scattered to the wind on the foothills of her beloved Mount Fujiyama, I still woke up feeling her hair on my face and the scent of her perfume, though she'd never set foot on the houseboat. Teri would not want to compete with a ghost, I reasoned. No one would.

Killian's concern was warranted, although I didn't like to admit it. Someone out there was gunning for me and I needed my head clear. Emotional entanglements made you careless and forget details. That could get you dead quickly.

I checked the rearview and backtracked a couple of times to make sure I wasn't followed. I arrived on the houseboat and sat on the aft deck.

A tiny mew reached my ears and I turned to find a gray and white cat standing on the edge of the dock. He was soaked to the skin. All cats looked pathetic when they were wet. He wasn't wearing a collar.

"Hi, there."

As soon as I made eye contact, he jumped onto my boat and began exploring, doubtlessly following his nose toward my food.

"Did you fall in the bay?"

He came slowly and warily in my direction. I broke off a bite of egg and tossed it toward him. He took a sniff before snapping it into his mouth.

I reached out to pet him. He hissed at me and sped underneath a deck chair, his back arched, tail raised, fur standing up.

"Easy, fella, I won't hurt you."

He watched me when I went into the kitchen and poured some milk into a saucer. I placed it near him; he tensed up and hissed until I sat back down.

Cautiously, he sidled out from under the chair, as stealthy as though he were alone in enemy territory. He sniffed at the milk and trained one eye on me for a moment.

"Go ahead, it's just milk."

He lapped it up. I watched him and the bay. The water

was a deep green-blue with a slight chop; a charter boat cruised by with several girls in bikinis and guys in surfing shorts. The girls waved. I waved back.

"Don't assume you can stay here," I said. "My wife liked cats. But she's gone. Besides, I live on a houseboat. Cats hate water. You'd be miserable here."

He wasn't paying me any attention now. The milk gone, he walked over; I slowly let my arm dangle, and he rubbed against my hand. I rubbed him back, eliciting a soft purr. I patted my lap and he jumped up. We sat there for a long time watching the water.

Finally, while the cat explored his new surroundings, I secured the boat before going to the stateroom. I went to bed after slipping the Glock beneath my pillow. I would need the rest. I had unsavory places to go.

13

Many consider Miami to be the ultimate in travel destinations. Television propels the myth of sun soaked beaches, beautiful girls in bikinis, handsome young men with chiseled bodies, all soaking up the sun. Nighttime is glamorous clubs filled with attractive people dancing and hooking up for evenings of hot romance. Reality can be a lot uglier.

The Scarlett Letter was a popular club located in an off-red deco-style building just a few blocks from South Beach. The two burly fellows standing watch at the velvet rope checked a clipboard, verified Teri and me, and motioned us through. We walked in through a set of double imitation wood doors with long brass handles. There was a large lobby with a snack bar and restrooms. I saw a few kids talking on cell phones. Even here, I could feel the pulsing bass of the music and a rear filling along my upper jaw began to throb.

"Where do you want me?" Teri asked. She was in night-club apparel: a velvet mini-dress, high heels, and a string of black pearls.

"Just monitor the door. Once I go through give me ten minutes. If I don't show, come in."

"I can do that."

I took a deep breath and went into the club. It was wall-to-wall people. The dance floor occupied the center of the room and tables on three different levels surrounded it. Here the music was louder and the throbbing of my filling intensified.

Bodies were everywhere. People were nearly sitting on top of one another and for the life of me, I couldn't understand being in such a place and trying to have a good time. There were all kinds here: gay, straight, and a few that I couldn't quite figure out. I maneuvered my way through the throng.

"Wanna dance, stud?" asked a drunken Oriental girl standing by the brass railing. She had on a tube top and a mini skirt gone so far north I could see she wasn't wearing underwear.

"Sorry, two left feet." I couldn't tell if she heard me. Maybe she wasn't even talking to me. She didn't answer one way or the other so I never knew.

Hidden out of the way from the revelers was a door discreetly marked EMPLOYEES ONLY. Another burly fellow who looked like a match to the twins outside stood just far enough away to make it look as though he wasn't guarding the door, but close enough that he could keep an eye on it. He sported a rocklike jaw and a shirt with the club name on it. The shirt strained against his barrel chest.

"Can I help you?"

"Here to see Carl," I said. "He's expecting me."

"Name?"

"Don Greer," I said in a Boston accent. "I spoke ta' him

on the phone yesterday." I handed him a business card that said I was an importer and distributor.

He unlocked the door with a pass card and motioned me through. I stepped into a hallway with thick shag and rosewood paneling. The door closed behind me and the club noise ceased completely. At the end of the hall was another door marked MANAGER. I walked in without knocking. The office was neat and smaller than I'd expected.

Carl Westland never really looked like a spy, which made him perfect for the trade. He was short and the years away from Langley had made him soft around the middle. He was balding on top and wore thick heavy rim glasses. He had his feet propped up on his desk, phone in hand.

"And just what the hell am I supposed to do? Tell the distributor that I have a client reserving this place in two weeks and he wants Beluga caviar. He's paying for it and I need it." He looked up and saw me and his face went a little white.

"I'll call you back," he said and slowly put the phone down.

"Hi, Carl." I walked around the room checking it for any surprises. "You look like you saw a ghost."

"How'd you get in here?"

I went into my Greer persona. "It was that easy. You don't remember talking with me yesterday?"

He shook his head in disgust. "I must be getting senile to fall for that crap. Get the hell out, Logan."

"Just a couple of questions."

"Go spit."

"Carl, Carl." I sat down in a comfortable chair placed in front of his desk. "After all we've been through together."

"Logan, I could get in real trouble. If they spot you in my club—"

"Who?"

"You know."

"I know that this club is a front for US intelligence gathering. You monitor the drug runners for the DEA, the situation in Cuba for the State Department, and everyone else for the FBI and NSA.

"Man's got to make a living, bubba."

"Agreed. I just need some info because you know everything. Did someone put a hit out on me?"

Carl snorted. "You don't know?"

"Tell me."

He shrugged. "Your whole team, Logan. The whole damn unit's been targeted."

"Why?"

"Rochelle. He was working on something."

"Are you saying Bill targeted us?"

"No. He was working on something that put someone's nose out of joint."

"What?"

"I don't know. Word is, Rochelle found something, something that shook him up pretty bad. He went to Langley with it—he was retired by then—and told them what he'd found. Then, all hell breaks loose." Carl leaned forward. "Look, spy boy, I've got two years until my pension and I've got a good gig here. Run the club, keep an eye on the local nasties, and work my sources, and the Beltway boys stay happy. Don't screw this up for me."

"What about James Forsythe?"

"He and Bill were on this thing together. I can't confirm it but I think Bill couldn't get any help from Langley so he subcontracted it out."

"To Forsythe."

Carl put his index finger to his nose. "The man had the means, money, and influence to get about anything done."

"What were they getting done?"

"I don't know. Word has it that it was something that certain people didn't want to leak out."

"What?"

"Who the hell knows? Whatever it was, the old man blew a gasket and went running off to Langley."

"You can find out. You have eyes and ears everywhere. Find out for me."

I heard a door slam down the hall and a moment later the office door banged open. The muscled fellow at the door who'd admitted me charged in, pistol drawn. He fired twice then I was on him, grabbed the gun arm by the wrist to secure the weapon, and judo flipped him onto Carl's desk. He held onto the pistol and fired when he landed; the bullet went by my head slamming into the far wall. I hammered his wrist downward into my knee and the pistol clattered to the floor. He rolled onto his feet.

I realized I had a problem when another bouncer burst through the door. I dove for the gun on the floor when the second bouncer jerked and I heard the sound of flesh on flesh. He spun and I saw a flash of Teri. She kicked him in the groin and executed a perfect jump kick, catching the bouncer square in the chest. The force hurtled him through the door, into the office, narrowly missing me, and against the wall. He bounced once, his head snapping back. His eyes rolled and he sank to the carpet.

First guy wasn't moving and I saw why. Teri had confiscated a Sig Sauer 9mm from somewhere and held it in a two-hand grip aimed right at center mass.

"Thanks," I said.

"I saw him take a call and charge in," Teri said. "Figured you might be in trouble." She looked at the bouncer and smiled. It wasn't a flirty smile; it was the smile that said 'I'm not afraid to shoot you if I need to and I'm okay with that.'

Carl wasn't there. I looked behind the desk to see him cowering under it.

"Damn bouncers..." he gasped. "Must work for them... Tried to be careful..."

"What's going on, Carl?"

The second bouncer scrambled to his feet and made a move toward me. Teri ran, slamming the butt of the pistol across the bouncer's skull and he toppled to the floor.

Teri said, "Let's get out of here. We're going to have company."

I couldn't agree more. I glanced at Carl. "What's going on?"

"Get going. We'll talk later if I'm still breathing. I'll see what I can find out."

We left quickly but calmly, walking out and driving off. Teri wiped the pistol off, took it apart, and threw the pieces one by one out the window.

"Thanks for not shooting the creep," I said.

"It was tempting, I admit."

"Someone made a phone call after I went in." I made another last-minute turn and checked the rearview. So far, there was no tail. After another forty-five minutes of aimless driving without a sign of being followed, I took I-95 north toward home.

My cell rang. Killian said, "People are searching your boat, bro."

"Where are you?"

"Hiding out three slips down. This is really a nice boat."

"Won't the owners mind?"

"They would if they were here," Killian said. "At the moment they're away for some cultural event."

"So, who's searching?"

"Two guys, suits and nice hardware."

"F.B.I.?"

"Who can tell?" Killian answered. "So many people want you dead right now I need a damn playbill to keep them all straight."

"How's Lucky?"

"Who's Lucky?"

"I just adopted a stray cat."

"Don't know and don't care. How'd things go in Miami?"

I relayed the events.

"Someone's keeping tabs on you, bro."

KILLIAN WAITED on the dock for us. I stepped onto the boat. Lucky came bounding out from beneath a deck chair and rubbed my leg.

"I hope you at least hissed at them or something," I told him.

"They didn't make any mess," Killian said. "That's the good part."

He was right. No mess, but I noticed that the occasional object that wasn't quite where it was when I left. Nothing bad, just enough to let me know they'd been there.

I looked at Killian. "How was it you were watching my boat?"

"I wasn't. Came by to see you. Saw them get on the boat when I got out of my car."

"You need a name for the boat," Teri said. "It's unlucky to have a boat with no name."

"Titanic had a name," Killian said. "Look what happened to it."

Teri shot him the finger. "You're supposed to be on my side."

I went to the galley where I procured pen and paper from a drawer. I wrote BUGGED? and showed it to them.

"I can't decide on a name. It's between *Hiyidoshi* and *Marlowe*."

"Neither one is all that appealing," Killian nodded and took off.

Teri went to the fridge and grabbed a beer. She sat that delicious rear onto a barstool and rested her elbows on the bar. "Let's talk about something else."

"Okay."

"How about you and me?"

My back was to her so she didn't see me close my eyes for a second. "What about us?"

"I think you know."

I bent down, took a beer out, and turned back to her. "Are you wanting to start things up again?"

"That's something I've been asking myself," she said. "It was easier to say no when I was on the other side of the country."

"But being here with me..."

She just nodded and drank a long pull.

"We had a good time together," I said. "It was a happy time for me."

"I think I hear a but coming."

"Shikira died last year. I'm not sure where I am emotionally about it."

"Meaning a woman can have your body but nothing else, right?"

"Pretty much it." I thought of Karen. For a second, I felt

afraid that she might develop something more for me than I could give back.

"I heard what you did after Paris," she said. "Pretty ballsy."

I shrugged.

"You should have called me. I would have helped."

"Didn't want you involved."

Teri finished her beer. "Things got too complicated for us, didn't they?"

"That they did. Especially when we had to work together. Besides, when this is over, you'll be going back to California and your job."

"I probably won't go back there."

"Why not?"

She dropped her gaze onto the countertop.

"What is it, Teri?"

She took a deep breath. "They made a play for me in L.A."

I stopped what I was doing. I couldn't say anything.

Teri took a deep breath. "The day after I learned that Gina had been killed, they snatched me as I got out of my car. Pulled me into a van. They couldn't drown me in the tub like her because that would be too coincidental, two women dead the same way. They took me out to the beach. Gonna drown me in the ocean. They had a surfboard and one of those body suits that surfers wear. They were going to make it look like I'd been surfing, been knocked out by the board and drowned. They had it all worked out." She shook her head and her voice cracked. "They wanted me to change into the suit right there in the van with them watching. Bastards."

A wave of anger surged in me and I had to push it aside. "So how'd you get away?"

"Well, I realized they hadn't sanitized the van enough so I stripped down to put on the wet suit. I started shaking and crying and pleading with them not to kill me. They were so busy looking at my boobs that they didn't see me snatch a screwdriver. I stabbed the one holding the gun and shot the other one. I wiped everything down, threw the pistol in the ocean, and fled L.A. One of them had mentioned your name, so I came to find you."

"What did he say about me?"

"That there was a Major in Florida next on the list." She was quiet for a moment. "I hadn't killed anyone in three years."

I knew the feeling. The laceration on my neck burned at the thought.

"It makes no sense," I said. "They try to kill you and Gina to make it look accidental but they flat out kill Bill and try the same with me. Doesn't make sense."

"Maybe there are two different sets of killers," Teri suggested.

"Or maybe that's what they're trying to make it look like."

I didn't say anything. I walked out onto the deck. Teri came out and stood beside me. The bay was a deep turquoise and a tugboat chugged by.

"I'm sorry I didn't tell you before."

"This is what made it so hard for us," I said. "We were selective on what we wanted the other to see and know."

"Occupational hazard," she said.

We were silent for a moment then Teri asked, "Do you want me to leave town?"

"No." I turned and put my arms around her. "I'm glad you're okay, Teri."

She responded and held me tight. "You, too."

Killian appeared. He had a hand-held electronic detector and went through the boat. It can take some time if you want to be thorough. He came onto the deck and opened his hand. There were three tiny devices in his palm, no larger than a pea.

"Living room, stateroom, and kitchen," Killian said. "Nicely placed."

Teri and I stared at the bugs.

"What the hell is going on?" Killian asked.

"I'm wondering the same thing."

"I hear Costa Rica is nice this time of year," Teri remarked.

It didn't sound like a bad idea.

14

I MET DERBY BY HIS POOL THE NEXT MORNING. THE GIRLS splashed in the water and some had decided swimwear was optional. Derby didn't seem to notice. I suppose you got used to it.

"My associate in Miami was quite upset by your inquiry," Derby said. "Considering that the Amber which you speak of was found dead in her apartment several days ago."

"Cause of death?"

"Heroin overdose, apparently. Her real name was Amanda Butler, if that helps, which is probably a moot point now."

A black hulk of a bodyguard, arms folded across his chest, towered near the edge of the patio. He looked at me through wraparound sunglasses but mostly he and Killian eyed each other like rival predators on the Serengeti.

"Any way I can talk to this associate?"

"That," Derby said, "Would not be a wise idea. You understand he's keeping a low profile right now."

"I understand, but it's just—"

Derby leaned forward on the table so we were almost nose-to-nose. "Listen, my cracker friend, I received an interesting phone call about you. Told me that you were trouble and to not get involved with you." Derby's eyes were emotionless orbs of darkest ebony. "I did this much because of Killian. Now the favor is repaid." He glanced over at Killian. "We square, Killian?"

"We're square." Killian never took his gaze from the bodyguard.

Derby nodded. "I don't need cops from any level knowing about me. Bad for business, you see. So get out. Don't come snooping around here again or I'm going to get upset."

Sometimes it's best to realize when you've worn out your welcome. I nodded. "I appreciate the help."

Derby didn't shake my hand.

"THEY'RE WATCHING your every move, bro." Killian said.

We stood by my car. I opened the hood and trunk. It took us nearly fifteen minutes of searching but I found it, fastened to the frame and squeezed into the small space near the oil pan. I pried it out and showed it to Killian.

"GPS tracking device," I said. "I think it's still working."

An elderly couple sporting thick Brooklyn accents and a nice Cadillac sedan had parked beside me. They were talking to one of the boat captains on the next pier. Probably interested in chartering his boat.

Killian took the tracking device and placed it underneath the rear fender of the Cadillac.

"Let the bastards chase that for a while," he said.

東

"I NEED A FAVOR."

Jake Ross looked up at me from behind his desk. "Really."

"It's about a girl found dead in Miami," I said. "Cause of death was ruled a heroin overdose. I don't think it was."

"Why does it matter?"

"The girl was Amber. Her real name was Amanda Butler."

Ross put down his pen and leaned back. "I know. I located her. Feds took her before I could get an interview with her."

"Can they do that?"

"Yes. I don't like it anymore than you do. Welcome to my world."

"There's something big going on here," I said. "My boat's been bugged, GPS trackers fixed to my car."

"And this is related to Forsythe's murder?"

"You tell me, Lieutenant. One more thing. There was a murder of a woman in L.A. Name was Gina Kennedy."

Ross wasn't stupid. "You think they're related?"

"Don't know until I get the facts."

"Okay, I have a friend with Miami Homicide. I'll give him a call. I'll get hold of L.A."

"Thanks, Lieutenant. I appreciate it."

Ross stared at me for a moment. "I have this gut feeling that things are going to start getting nasty around you, Logan."

I HAD to wait twenty minutes before I could see Karen.

Finally, her door opened and a short balding man walked out. He didn't even look at me. Karen motioned me in and I sat down.

Karen moved behind her desk. "Anything new on the case?"

I told her about Amber. "I have a friend on the police department trying to get me the details."

"He gives you any flack, let me know," Karen said. "I'll get the report."

"You may need to find another detective."

"Why?"

I shook my head. "Things are getting complicated. I'm getting bugged, tracking devices on my car, and all our witnesses are turning up dead."

"You don't seem like the kind of man who'd let that bother him."

"I think the feds are doing it, Karen."

"They can't do that."

"Someone is. And I don't know if it's related to this case or not." I sighed. "I think Forsythe's murder may have something to do with another series of events going on. It goes back to my old unit. Several others in my unit have died. It may be related to Forsythe's death, but maybe not. I just don't know yet. But if the feds keep pressing, I may not be able to devote my attention to Tracy."

"Does it involve your intelligence days?"

"Tracy's father is dead, as are some of those who worked with him. There's a connection there but I can't find it."

"You said that Tracy's father was once your boss."

"Yes."

"So he commanded your unit."

"Yes."

I saw in her eyes that she was working the logic out, trying to find connections.

"Can you tell me about it?"

"No," I said. "I can't."

I think a pang of hurt flashed in her eyes but it was gone immediately. Maybe I was wrong.

東

"AMANDA BUTLER WAS FOUND dead by her landlord," Ross said the next morning. He plopped down in my deck chair and we sat and watched the water. "There was a massive amount of horse in her—more than enough to kill her."

"Suicide?"

Ross shrugged. "No note. Friends say she never mentioned killing herself or seemed depressed."

"Accidental?"

"That's what the M.E.'s report said," Ross replied. "I talked to the doc who did the autopsy. I asked him if there was any proof of a drug history—track marks, etc. The file didn't show any. He said that there was evidence of coke and grass in her system. The septum in her nose showed evidence of erosion."

"But no heroin."

"None. So the theory is she tried it once and it killed her. Like that college basketball star a few years back. Tried coke for the first time and threw him into cardiac arrest. It happens, Logan."

"What about the L.A. case?"

"Gina Kennedy was thirty-nine, a successful marketing agent with a big firm out there. She was found in her bathtub under the water dead. A hypodermic needle was still in her arm."

"No history of drug abuse."

"None. Her work did random drug testing of its employees regularly. She came up clean every time." Ross took a breath and rubbed his chin. "You know, Logan, I never went to the University, just a small community college here to get my bachelor's. Only way to advance in rank anymore in police work. Didn't do that until I was almost forty. So I may not have an Ivy League degree but I can't help but see some similarities here."

"Then you're as smart as I thought you were, Lieutenant."

"Who's the Kennedy girl?"

"She worked with me once."

"She was a spy?"

"Operative. I commanded her in the field."

"Post mortem says there was evidence of a struggle."

"So how did the M.E. rule it an O.D?"

"Feds came in and took over the case," Ross said. "I talked to a buddy of mine out there, Dave Fletcher. We worked together on nabbing a guy here wanted for a triple homicide in L.A. once. He worked your friend's case. Said the feds came in and shut the whole thing down."

"Now you see."

"An hour ago I got a call from the boss. Feds are screaming at him about my inquiries. He then screamed at me."

"Did you tell anyone?"

"No," Ross said. "I knew better than that."

"Yet they knew."

Ross sighed. "I don't know what the hell you stumbled upon, Logan, but it's making a lot of powerful forces nervous."

"I'm sorry, Lieutenant. I didn't mean to get you in trouble."

Ross waved it away. "I'm a cop. This is what I do. And I don't like being told I can't do it." He walked over to the railing. "One more thing. There was a partial print recovered at the Kennedy girl's apartment. It matched one of two bodies they found on the beach. They'd been stabbed with a sharp instrument. M.E. said a screwdriver or something similar. They'd been stuffed in a van and everything had been wiped clean. Know anything about that?"

I shook my head. "They think the dead guy was responsible for killing Gina?"

"Fletcher thinks so, but again the Feds told him not to worry about it."

"Lieutenant, if the dead guy killed Gina, then I won't shed any tears over him. She was a good lady and a great operative."

Ross grunted. "Whoever took them out was good, that's for sure."

"Sounds like it."

"I also heard that you hang out with a guy named Killian."

"We went through Special Forces together."

"You know him well?"

"No one knows Killian well. He's a private person."

"Maybe he has reason to be."

"What's your point, Lieutenant?"

"Nothing at all. Just making sure you don't get involved with people who make my job busier."

"Killian's a straight up guy. He's saved my life a few times."

"Just making sure you know." Ross threw the empty bottle in the trash and stepped off onto the dock.

"Lieutenant?"

Ross turned around.

"Just so there's no misunderstanding between us. We both know that things might get bloody before it clears up. I left that life a long time ago. I don't want trouble, but I will defend myself."

Ross seemed to let the words sink in for a moment. He nodded. "Since we're sharing, Logan, let me share something, too. You step over the line and I'll see to it that the state yanks your license so fast you won't be able to blink. Then I'll put the cuffs on you myself." He turned and walked to his car. I watched him go.

Lucky came from under a chair and rubbed against my hand.

"When everything hits the fan, buddy, you better make sure you get a good hiding spot."

15

Ross barely had time to get out of the parking lot when FBI Special Agents Healey and Barlow appeared on the dock. I was in my favorite chair on the foredeck reading the comics.

"May we come aboard?" Healey asked.

"Depends on what you want. I haven't read Dilbert yet."

"We need to talk," Barlow answered.

"You should have called. I promised you coffee last time."

"This is not a social visit, Mr. Logan." Barlow stepped onto the boat. "You're in serious trouble."

"Is it for tossing the listening devices you planted overboard or removing the GPS tracking device from my car?"

"I don't know what you're talking about." Barlow towered over me.

"Careful, Agent Barlow, I get nauseous when I'm scared."

"Let me tell you something, Logan, I mean it when I say to quit snooping into this mess."

"And what mess would that be? I have several at the moment."

"Ok, smart ass, on your feet. You're under arrest."

I didn't get up. "For what?"

"Obstruction of justice, interfering with a federal investigation, resisting arrest. How's that for starters?"

"Barlow, you couldn't pin that on me with a riveter," I said, glancing at Healey. "Is he serious?"

"Stan, calm down," Healey said. "We're here to talk."

"You can't talk to these clowns," Barlow said. His face reddened and he looked like he might blow a gasket. "There's only one thing that gets their attention." He reached down and grabbed my shirt. "On your feet, shit head—"

I could have taken him easily. There were a hundred ways to do it and he would have been on the floor in various levels of hurt. But I wasn't that stupid. Barlow cuffed me, searched me, and threw me in the back of the car. I was taken downtown to the Federal building and the Bureau's office where I was processed. I got one phone call. I called Karen.

They stuck me in a holding cell awaiting transport to the county jail. I was alone so I lay down on the bed and napped. One thing they teach you is when you're in a situation you can't control, sleep and eat when you can. You never know when you'll have the next chance. I didn't have to wait long.

Within thirty minutes, Karen was at the cell door along with an older gentleman in a nice dark suit. He had a gun on his hip and looked to be the senior agent in charge of the office. He looked like a whipped pup. Karen kept giving him sharp glances.

"And I want all of my employee's belongings re-turned to him immediately," Karen said as the agent unlocked the cell. "I will be speaking with Washington this afternoon."

"It was just a simple misunderstanding, Ms. Lords."

"How about the listening devices planted on Mr. Logan's boat? Did the Bureau have a wiretap warrant to do that?"

"I assure you the Bureau had nothing to do with that—"

"Well I'm checking into this situation," Karen said. "Mr. Logan is a licensed private investigator hired by my firm to investigate false allegations against a client. If the Bureau continues to harass him, Harry, I assure you I will fry your ass in court after I splash this all over the six-o'clock news!" She turned and walked with me out to a window where another agent returned my personal possessions. I verified everything was there, signed the release. I saw Healey at a desk. She glanced at me. I didn't see Barlow.

We walked out into the sunshine. "Thanks, Karen."

"Assholes. Barlow is being reprimanded as we speak."

"I wanted to deck the officious ass."

"That wouldn't have been a good idea."

"I know."

"Are you sure they were the ones who planted the bugs?"

"I don't know," I said. "One of my associates said they were two men in suits."

"Could have been Bureau," Karen said.

I nodded. "And maybe not. I have to talk to someone who might know. Right now there's something else I want to check out."

We made a stop at my houseboat then drove to her office. It took me only a few minutes of scanning with a detector before I found them.

"One in your phone," I said, "And another in your desk lamp." I held them up.

I saw her jaw clench. "Sonofabitch."

I scanned her reception area, much to the surprise of the two women stationed there but found nothing more.

"Are they still on?"

"No. They're designed to shut down once they've been removed from the surface they're attached to."

"So who did this?"

"That's what I'm going to find out," I said. "Watch yourself."

"You, too."

東

"PRETTY NICE," Teri said, admiring one of the bugs from Karen's office. "Identical to the ones on your boat."

"I need you to contact Mel in D.C. See what he can tell you."

"Is he still around?"

"According to Killian, yes. Still in business at the old spot."

"You know him better than I do."

I winked. "But he'll be more apt to do the favor for you."

"He will?"

"He always said you had a nice rack."

Teri rolled her eyes. "Men are all alike."

"Keep low in D.C., Teri."

"I know. Eyes are everywhere." She kissed me on the cheek. "I'll get packed and leave. Is Karen paying for this?"

"Yes, considering the bugs we're checking out were in her office."

She smiled. "First class."

I watched that nice rear walk out and wondered if I was sending her to her death. It would not be the first time I'd sent men to die, or the first time that some of them had met their eternal fate then. However, it was never easy for anyone who commanded men unless he was a callous bastard, and those usually didn't last. Recent events had made me paranoid nearly to the point of silliness. I was seeing shadows everywhere and suspecting everyone except Killian and Teri. Paranoia is a great tool to have in covert ops but it is a double-edged sword. A paranoid person can be gotten to. Play on his paranoia, reinforce it, and a skilled operative can make him dance like a puppet until its time to strike.

Night fell across the bay. The water was calm; the sunset was a mix of orange and reds that made the city skyline glow. I sat on the upper deck while Lucky lay on an old blanket that he'd claimed.

I sat and thought. I seemed to have pieces of the puzzle but lacked the interlocking ones that made them fit together:

Bill had stumbled onto something. I didn't know what it was but it was information of some kind. Bill runs to Langley and tells them. For whatever reason, Langley blows him off, ignores him, or gives him the bureaucratic runaround.

Then the plot gets fuzzy. Either Bill goes to Forsythe for help and thus triggers the killing of his old unit members, or the killings happen first and pushes Bill to desperately seek out help—Forsythe, in this case—and thus sets in motion heir own demises.

It was all I had and until I found out more, anything further was merely hypothesis and supposition.

I caught movement at the corner of my eye. Agent Healey stood on the dock looking up at me.

"Can I come on board?"

"Did you bring Melvin Purvis with you?"

"No."

"Come aboard."

She did then looked around. "How do I get up there?"

I pointed. "Ladder."

She climbed up with ease and sat on a deck chair.

"I like the view," she said.

"So how is your partner doing?"

"He's not happy. He got a royal chewing out from the boss. I got a warning but the chief knows I'm junior partner and he also knows that Stan can get a little carried away with his temper." She looked around. "You have beer on this hulk?"

"I take it you're off duty."

"You would be correct."

I had a small cooler already loaded and handed her a bottle. She nodded thanks and took a large swallow. "I needed that."

"Glad to be of help."

She said, "I'm sorry about the whole thing. I really am."

"What's the Bureau's interest in James Forsythe?"

"That is a matter of national security and cannot be discussed."

"Tracy Rochelle didn't kill Forsythe," I said. "The Bureau would let an innocent girl go to jail for murder to protect national security?"

"You are so sure she's innocent?"

"Agent Healey, Tracy is a drug user and somewhat lax in her restraint, but she couldn't have killed Forsythe. That girl doesn't know one end of a katana from another."

"Anyone can stick a blade into someone."

"Not that way. It requires some skill, especially to run it through the body and into the bed. If you tried it, the blade would probably get stuck partway through. To do it the way it was done required someone who knew something about using a sword. Tracy was simply in no state to do it."

"I think you're wrong."

I got up. "Then let me prove it. Come on."

Once we were on the lower deck, I brought out two melons and a katana in its lacquered *saya*.

"Where did you get that?"

"It was a gift to me from my first sensei when I left Japan," I said. "It is part of what we call the *daisho*, the twin swords worn by the samurai in feudal Japan. Only a samurai could wear both swords. This one is the katana, the primary weapon of a samurai, his heart and soul. The shorter sword —the *wakizashi*—was used as a back-up weapon as well as for committing seppuku."

"You mean hara-kiri?"

I shook my head. "That is a bastardized term. The ninja were said to commit hara-kiri since they were assassins and did not live by the code of bushido. But in the end, it's the same thing—ritualized suicide." I withdrew the katana in a single motion and swiveled it, handing it to Healey grip first. "I'm not supposed to do this, but I need to make a point. Be careful, the blade's sharp. It'll easily take your finger off."

She took the sword in both hands, holding it clumsily, trying to adopt a posture like the one she had seen on TV or the movies. To the untrained eye, she looked fine. To me, she looked awkward and laughable but I said nothing.

"Since you've handled firearms you must have good eye hand coordination," I said. "I'm going to toss this melon in the air—just a light toss. Take the sword and chop it in half."

"Sounds easy."

"Ready?"

She nodded.

I gave the melon an easy toss. She brought the blade

down and struck. The sword sliced into the melon and stuck. I pried it loose.

"See?"

I took the sword and wiped the blade. "Toss me the other melon."

She hesitated before picking up the other one. She tossed it and I flashed the katana out. It took less than a second. The melon fell to the deck in four pieces.

Agent Healey looked at it. I saw she was thinking things over.

"See? It took some skill to kill James Forsythe like that. Not a lot, but more skill than Tracy Rochelle had." I wiped the sword clean again and never took my eyes off her while I sheathed the blade.

"You could have killed him."

"Yes, but I didn't. I wouldn't have killed him like that."

"How would you have done it?"

"He was killed that way by someone wanting to make a point," I said. "Killing was an art in feudal Japan. So was making love. Just as much as painting or poetry. The killer wanted to send a message."

"What kind of message?"

"One, he's trained in the martial arts, secondly, that Forsythe had made powerful enemies."

"I heard a tale once," Healey said. "About some samurai who avenged their lord then killed themselves."

I nodded. "The forty-seven ronin."

"Ronin?"

"A ronin was a master-less samurai. A samurai lived to serve his lord. When a lord died, the samurai who served him either had to die himself or find another lord. When they could not find another lord to serve, they would often kill themselves rather than be ronin, a samurai without a lord. Some became swords for hire.

"The forty-seven samurai served a lord who was betrayed and murdered by another lord. Since they were sworn to protect their lord, the samurai were disgraced. For three years, they lived as thieves, beggars, even mad men, but waiting and plotting. One night they attacked, sneaking into the castle and killing their lord's betrayer. Once it was done, they knelt in the courtyard of the castle and committed seppuku for they had lived to serve their lord and once that need was gone, they had nothing else to live for."

"I don't understand," Healey said.

I smiled. "Yes, you do. You serve something greater than yourself. You serve the Bureau and America."

"You did, too, at one time."

"Yes. Serving God and country was my life, my calling, my profession. In the end, I was a disillusioned man and so I walked away." I returned the sword to its place on the low teakwood table inside and came back out. She was still thinking things over.

"What did Bill Rochelle find?"

She closed her eyes.

"Agent Healey, I want to help, but I have to know what's going on. Members of my unit are dead. They were friends of mine. I served with them."

"General Rochelle found some information," she said. "Information that sent Langley scrambling."

"What was it?"

"All we know is that it concerned the Paris bombing last year where 12 people died. Including your wife."

My blood ran cold. "Tell me. Why did Langley turn him down?"

"We don't know. Apparently the information connected someone high up in the government."

"So how does the Bureau know anything about it?"

"Gina Kennedy. She contacted me two days before she died. Rochelle had confided in her."

"How did you know Gina?"

"We grew up together," Healey said.

"Really?"

She nodded. "Gina was supposed to meet me in Oklahoma City to tell me everything. Said she didn't want to talk about it on the phone. Before the meeting, she was murdered. So this is personal to me, too."

"Did Gina say anything at all?"

"Only that members of her old unit were being killed and that she had evidence. It led me to Bill Rochelle. Now, Amanda Butler was killed the same way as Gina. And Bill and Forsythe knew each other. It's all linked somehow." She stretched. "I want to solve this case. I think it's related to Forsythe's murder."

"You have an interesting way of doing it, Agent Healey. The Bureau has arrested and charged an innocent girl with murder, made false conclusions contrary to crime scene and autopsy photos, and—"

"Logan, all that was done to protect the investigation," Healey said. "We're not stupid—we know that whoever is involved has eyes and ears out there. We needed to make them think they were safe, that we were barking up the wrong tree. We know that Gina Kennedy was murdered; we know that Tracy Rochelle is innocent. Right now, jail might be the safest place for her." For a moment, the tough police countenance threatened to burst. "Gina and I were close friends back home. It hurt me when we had to write that she OD'd. But we had to do it." She took another swig of beer. "I want to find the bastards responsible."

"So do I."

She nodded. "We need to find out what Bill Rochelle discovered."

"Any thoughts on how we do that?"

"The trail seems to be getting colder."

"I'm doing everything I can."

"You might be the only one who can," she said, bitterness in her voice. "The Bureau is being hamstrung by someone. I don't know who." She handed me the empty beer bottle and stood. "Keep in touch, Logan."

She walked away and left me alone with my thoughts.

It has something to do with Paris.

I thought that part was over. I'd gotten the information and stormed all over the globe to find those responsible.

A beautiful day in Paris. We had left the hotel, walked the block to the little café, and sat down. Her dark eyes gleamed at me from across the table. I spotted the flower vendor across the street. He had a pushcart and moved slowly down the sidewalk.

A sudden urge made me get up and battle the early morning traffic to cross the street. I turned to see Shikira staring at me, smiling.

I'd noticed the man with the briefcase sit down at the table beside us. Now the table was empty, the briefcase sitting beneath it. I spotted the back of the man making a hasty retreat.

I remember screaming out a warning to her a moment before the briefcase exploded. The blast ripped through the café, the concussion wave throwing me against and over the flower cart....

I had traced the bomber and those who were behind it. And I'd killed them. From a flat in London to a dive bar in Mexico, to a D.C. brownstone. It had been an attempt on my life. Except I had moved. Driven by Fate or forces unknown to leave my seat in those few seconds to distance myself from the blast.

Bill had discovered something new about Paris. Something that had unnerved him, enough to make him go fill in Langley. What was it? Had I missed someone?

I thought I had gotten them all. Maybe, just maybe, I was wrong.

16

Bill always preached that intelligence is a puzzle. You took pieces of information and put them together to get the bigger picture. Sometimes the pieces you used could be flawed or downright bad.

What I'd perceived as the feds willingness to railroad an innocent girl was actually a clever smokescreen to hide the actual investigation. I'd been dead wrong about the Bureau, although I hated to admit it to myself at the time.

Healey denied any knowledge of the Bureau planting the listening devices on my boat. I believed her. I didn't want to but I did. She also didn't know about the men who'd followed me into the mall. She promised to check into it.

I pulled into Karen's driveway. The ocean roared nearby and people crowded the beach. Karen met me at the door. Her normal demeanor, calm and professional, was gone. Her eyes were puffy and red.

"What's wrong?"

"Come here. In the garage." I followed her through a side door and into a two-car garage.

"I went shopping and came back and found this—"

I spotted the dead cat on the floor. It lay in a pool of blood and I could tell it had been shot in the head.

"I didn't know you had a cat."

"I don't. It belongs to the neighbors. It hangs out over here sometimes. I put out a little food for it."

"When you left, did you close the garage door?"

"Yes."

"Was he in here then?"

"No," she said. "Someone brought him in here and killed him."

"You need to call the cops."

"This was a warning, wasn't it?"

I didn't look at her. "Certainly seems that way." I got my cell phone and dialed Ross. Then I dialed Healey.

"WE'RE DUSTING FOR PRINTS," Ross said. "Did you touch anything?"

"We came in through the side door," I said. "I don't think I touched the knob."

"Probably a waste of time. Anyone with a half a mind would use gloves." Ross turned and watched the Crime Scene Unit technicians dusting all the applicable areas.

The garage door was up and another car pulled into the already crowded driveway. Healey got out. Ross gave a slight groan.

"Who called her?"

I raised my hand. "I did."

"Why would you do that?"

"Although her partner's an ass, she's not. She wants to solve this thing."

Healey came up. Ross briefed her. "Are you taking over this case, too, Agent Healey?"

"That won't be necessary, Lieutenant. I'm sure your boys are doing a fine job."

She went over to Karen, now sitting on a lawn chair. Ross and I moved a little farther away.

"I want to get a look at Forsythe's beach house."

"Why?"

"I don't know. I'm at a dead end. Maybe I can find something."

"Doesn't sound like much of a plan."

"It's better than going home and drinking," I said.

"Not really." Ross gave a tiny nod toward Healey. "Better ask her if you want to go there."

"I would. I trust her but I don't trust anyone else with her. I want you to tag along just to make sure I don't do anything illegal."

"You're already doing something illegal."

"I mean something really bad."

Ross opened his mouth to retort but stopped when Healey joined us. "You'll let me know if you find anything, Lieutenant." She asked.

"Of course."

Healey gave me a glance before walking to her car and driving away.

"What the hell," Ross said. "I've nothing to lose but my pension." He nodded toward his unmarked car. "Come on."

I promised Karen I'd check in on her later, got into the car, and we took off toward the house where James Forsythe died.

The beach house looked much as it did when I first saw it. The crime scene tape was gone, the ocean still roared just beyond the beach, and even the BMW was still there.

"The door's locked," Ross said.

"No, it's not. It's unlocked," I answered. "Will you just look how beautiful the ocean is today?"

"Believe I will," Ross said, turning his back to me and gazing at the blue water. It took me thirty seconds but there was soft click and Ross stepped back into view. I swung the door open. "See? Unlocked."

"I'll be," he answered.

As though reading each other's minds we headed to the bedroom. The feds had cleaned up the blood but there were still dark stains on the mattress that would probably never come out. There was also the tear. Here, James Forsythe had lived his final moments of life as someone ran a sword through him.

"M.E. says he struggled some," Ross said. "It wasn't quick."

"Running the sword through him required some skill. It also had to happen really fast. The killer couldn't have known how long Tracy would be. He had to put the sword through him and get away."

"Just like that?"

"Exactly like that. And no, it wasn't quick and painless for Forsythe."

"If that holds true then only two people could be the killer: Tracy or this Amber girl," Ross surmised. "Unless Forsythe was exploring new avenues with this Frank."

"Any rumors of Forsythe being bi?"

"Nope, straight hetero as far as we can tell."

"Okay, so Amber gets on board and kills him. Why?"

"You're the intelligence man. Any thoughts?"

"It's a pro job, Jake. A contract perhaps."

Ross snorted derisively. "And we have a phone book full of people who'd want to hire her to kill him."

"Amber got hired by a local pimp. Hard to believe that she'd be a killer posing as a hooker, especially if she was in a stable of girls."

Ross sighed. Amber wasn't the killer. She was a hooker and if Forsythe had been shot, stabbed, or poisoned, perhaps Amber would be a suspect. Running someone through with a katana...no. A hooker wouldn't do that.

There was a chair beside the dresser. I sat and looked around. It was a good theory but something was missing. Some element and I didn't know what it was. There were a hundred ways to kill someone and the way this was carried out didn't look to be random. It happened here for a reason.

I glanced at the closet and went over to take a closer look.

"There were at least four people in the house that we know of," I said. "Forsythe, Tracy, Frank, and Amber, no one else."

"Right."

Now let's suppose none of them were the killer. That means the killer had to sneak into the house without being seen."

"Possible if he knows what he's doing."

"He comes in to make the hit, but Forsythe's in the bed having sex with Tracy. The killer can't kill her, too—she's supposed to be the fall guy. And he can't let Tracy see him."

"He struck when Tracy went to the bathroom," Ross said. "So how would he know the time was right to strike?"

"He was watching. From this closet."

Ross stepped inside and closed the bi-fold doors. "He was waiting here. He could have snuck in and hid in the closet. He watched Forsythe and Tracy. When Tracy went to the head, he came out."

"Sex slows the reflexes," I added. "Forsythe was probably lying there, eyes closed, maybe even drifting off. He'd had a full evening."

"He was an inspiration." Ross opened the doors and stepped toward the bed. "Three steps and he would be in position, I think." He made the motion of stabbing a sword down. "How long would it take?"

"Less than thirty seconds. Plunge in the sword and he could leave."

Ross looked around as though checking for flaws in the theory. "I'd like to know who this Frank is."

"I think this Frank guy was Hardaway," I said. "As in Franklin Hardaway."

"You mean Senator Hardaway?"

"The same," I answered. "Hardaway chairs the Commerce subcommittee that overseas foreign trade and acquisitions. Forsythe needed Hardaway's approval to buy any overseas company."

"MicroCorp."

"You know about that."

"We do have some brains in the police force, Logan." Ross sighed. "Jesus, now you're telling me that a U.S. Senator is a murder suspect."

"You're the cop, you tell me."

"And if the Bureau suspects, I wonder if they'd try to get the Rochelle girl to make an I.D. that it was Hardaway?"

"She's not been asked as far as I know."

"It might explain the Bureau's interest."

"It could."

Ross thought a moment. "So, you think Hardaway came here to kill Forsythe?"

"No, he wouldn't be that stupid," I said. "Hardaway didn't kill him."

"You seem to be certain. You know the Senator?"

"We've crossed paths before."

"Could he have had it done?"

"That's a possibility," I said. "Oh, hell, Jake, we're just theorizing. Until we get something concrete, I'm spinning my wheels here."

We searched the house although we knew we wouldn't find anything. We checked everything we could think of. And we found nothing that might tell us more of what happened that night. If James Forsythe had any big secrets, either on Hardaway or anyone else, we couldn't find it.

"Maybe, if Forsythe did have something, he wouldn't have put it here. Maybe it's somewhere else." Ross said.

"Maybe," I said. "But if he brought Hardaway here to show him the evidence..."

Ross shook his head. "Forsythe needed Hardaway to pass his deal through Congress to buy MicroCorp. We all know how you do that in D.C. Forsythe invites Hardaway here to talk business and throws Amber in for a nice gift."

"A bribe," I said.

"Judging from Tracy's testimony, Hardaway partook of the bribe."

"Or a setup," I said. "Maybe he took some photos of Hardaway having a nice threesome with Tracy and Amber. With Hardaway running for President in a couple of years, it would have been good stuff to hang over his head to make sure the MicroCorp deal went through."

Ross nodded. "Lots of ways of doing it."

"Let's go," I said. "We're wasting our time here."

We got back in the car. Ross drove and we headed home. We didn't say anything for a long time. We were both thinking about the scenarios and the possibilities. Lines were emitting from all the players connecting to each other. We didn't know why.

Jake's eyes darted to the rearview mirror.

"What's up?"

He frowned. "Car's been following us. Moving up fast."

I turned and saw the black sedan coming up on our left. The windows were heavily tinted and something about the way the car moved let me know that there was a lot of horsepower and metal beneath the black chassis.

The rear window rolled down and I caught the flash of metal.

"Gun!" I yelled as the first shot ripped through the window.

17

IT WAS ONE OF THOSE SEMI-AUTO SHOTGUNS THAT CAN butcher anything in its path. The back driver's window shattered and a shudder went through our car. Two more shots boomed out. Fragments of seat cushion and chipped metal flew around us.

"Son of a—" Ross managed to yell and punched the accelerator. He headed for the freeway.

"No, he's got the horsepower to kill us there," I said. "Try the side streets. He's heavier and less maneuver-able."

Ross nodded and spun the wheel; the car did a hard right onto a side street. We were in a residential neighborhood and I hated like hell for anyone unlucky enough to be around but it was still better than the freeway. The sedan slowed to make the turn. It got on the street and accelerated. A boom and another shiver rippled through the vehicle.

"Any weapons in this piece of junk?"

"Don't you have your weapon?"

"I do," I answered. "But I was hoping for something a little more powerful."

Ross nodded, "Shotgun in the trunk."

"Wonderful."

"Flip the backseat down, dumb ass."

"Just keep them off our ass for a minute." I unbuckled my seatbelt and climbed in the back. Ross made another tight turn and I ended up ass over teakettle on the floorboard, cursing Ross and the whole situation.

"Get the damn gun! I can't keep them off forever!"

"I'd be most happy too if you'd be so kind as to hold the damn car steady."

There was a small strap on the back seat. I reached up and yanked. The back of the seat flipped down and I rolled up onto it, careful to keep myself from popping up in the rear window. There was a standard police issue Remington 870 12-gauge pump in the trunk. I grabbed it and jacked a shell in the chamber.

"Hope this thing has more than one shell."

"It does."

"If you're wrong I won't get to say I told you so."

"Here they come," Ross said. His face was a grim mask.

The sedan came up on the right side. I lay flat on my back, shotgun vertical on my chest, muzzle pointing toward my feet. A blast filled my ears and the passenger window shattered, spraying glass over me and the back seat. Ross cursed. He made another turn and I heard the other car turn with us. The engine revved. They were moving in for the kill.

"Logan, you are one cool mother."

Right. My palms were sweaty. I had that old tightness in my gut I'd experienced in the olden days and I suddenly realized that I'd missed it. The thought excited and terrified me. I'd sworn to leave that life behind—

"Just let me know when they're in position."

"Not yet..." Ross said.

Things slowed down in that way it always does when you're in a high tense situation. An old drive-thru wrapper lay on the floorboard. My pulse sounded in my ears. I smelled cologne. It wasn't mine. Ross's? I didn't have time to figure it out. I saw the top part of the sedan's roof, easing closer alongside us. A deep breath. Any minute now...

"Now!"

There was no more time to think. I sat up. Glass rained off me, the shotgun pointed out the window. I saw it all in an instant. The sedan was alongside, the rear driver's window was down, and I caught the fleeting image of a hard face looking at me from behind his weapon before I unloaded. The first blast went right through the open window and the hard face disappeared from view. My next shot hit the driver's side window, which took the blast without shattering. Bullet resistant, I thought, and then shot the tires. The sedan swerved as Ross took a hard left and I watched the sedan swerve again, this time too hard. It went on its side, spun into a parked car and ended up on its roof in the middle of Bowles Street.

We came to a halt and Ross shut off the engine. He looked over at me and then glanced back at the over-turned car.

"Son of a bitch," he said. He grabbed the radio mike from the floor where it had fallen and called for backup.

I SAT on the fender of a black and white sipping a cup of coffee and staring at my feet. Crime scene and forensics people scurried about. I was too tired to pay them any attention.

A pair of scuffed loafers filled my vision and I raised my

head to see a beefy cop in blue slacks and a jacket that didn't quite match. His tie was askew and he looked at me as if I'd just been convicted of shooting my mother. His badge shone from the holder on his belt and he had a snub-nosed .38 in a hip holster.

"Logan?"

"That's me."

"I'm Captain Albergray, Homicide Division."

"Nice to meet you, Captain."

He sat on the fender beside me. "What happened here?"

"Lt. Ross and I were shot at by some guys in the sedan." I pointed to it to emphasize my point. "They kept shooting and I shot back."

"What were you doing with Lt. Ross?"

"I believed I had some relevant information concerning the murder of James Forsythe but I didn't want to turn it over to the feds until I knew it was legit. Lt. Ross allowed me to go with him to check it out. On our return these bozos showed up."

"And the information?"

"Ross showed me that it was irrelevant. You guys had already covered that base."

He looked at me, wondering what to make of my story. Finally, he said, "Do you know those men in the sedan?"

"I didn't really get a look at them. Just their shotgun."

"No ID's on them," Albergray said as though I hadn't answered. "Probably pros. Ex-military. You capped one of them pretty good. We'll run their prints."

I nodded and looked back down at my shoes.

"Car was armored and built for this kind of work. What do you think about that?"

"Sounds like they planned it pretty well."

"Wonder who they were trying to hit, Logan? You or Ross?"

"I don't think they were being that choosey, Captain."

"Ross says you're an interesting fellow."

"I have a good press agent."

"I don't like my city streets turning into a shooting gallery," he said.

"I can understand that."

"I appreciate your efforts and helping out my man, Logan. Just don't think that gives you carte blanche in my town."

"I'll keep that in mind, Captain."

He tried giving me a hard look. Finally, he chuckled and walked back toward the car that sat upside down in the street.

Ross came over a minute later. "I see you met the boss."

"Yeah, he's going on my Christmas card list."

"He's okay," Ross said. "He's going to let our story hold."

"At least something is going right for me today."

"Thanks for saving my can, Logan."

"Forget it. I was saving my own as well."

"I mean it," Ross said. "I owe you one."

"I don't keep scores." I shrugged. "Am I free to go?"

"Yeah, let me get you a ride." Ross looked out at the overturned car. "What a mess."

18

When I got home, Teri was on the foredeck. She wore a blue string bikini and was giving Lucky a nice belly rub. He seemed to enjoy it.

"Glad you made yourself at home."

She started to smile, but turned it off. "What happened to you?"

"What?"

"Your face."

I found a mirror. I had several minor cuts, the largest being on my right temple near my eye. Teri took me to the head where she cleaned and dressed my wounds.

"Wanna talk about it?"

I told her about Karen, the cat, and the beach house. By the time I finished the shootout she was done with my face. I grabbed a beer and joined her on deck.

"How was D.C.?"

"Humid, crowded, and eyes everywhere," she said.

"How's Mel?"

"Relieved to know you're still alive and kicking. He sends his best."

"What did he tell you?"

Teri sighed. "The bugs are state of the art micro-circuitry. Not something used by the FBI. These are newer, definitely custom made, and cost a pretty penny to build. You plant one of these in any of your rooms, they'll pick up anything that goes on and then some."

"Who has the technology to build something like this?"

"Only a select few companies. Mostly Japanese, according to Mel. But there is one company that can do it that I found very interesting. They're already developing the next generation micro-electronics." She paused, waiting. "Care to guess?"

"MicroCorp?"

She nodded. "MicroCorp."

I picked up my cell and called Healey. She answered on the second ring.

"What do you know about MicroCorp?"

"Why do you want to know?"

"Because some of their fancy electronics were found on my boat and in Karen Lords' office."

Silence on the line for a moment then she said, "Tracy's attorney?"

"Precisely. Is it coincidence that someone murders Forsythe just as he's trying to buy MicroCorp then uses their equipment to bug my houseboat?"

"I see your point," Healey said. "I'll get back to you."

"So, what the hell does it mean?"

Killian stood in my galley. He drew a knife from my butcher's block, twirled it easily between his fingers, and set to work chopping an onion. Teri sat on the sofa, headphones in her ears, working the New York Times crossword.

"Let's see if I have this straight," Killian said. The knife was almost a blur. "Forsythe was buying Micro-Corp. Micro-Corp possibly made the bugs that were planted on your boat and in Karen's office."

"Nice summary."

"Everything's connected to everything else. So why don't we know what the hell is going on?"

"It all hinges on that intel Bill found," I said. "Until we find it, we're only getting bits and pieces."

"Okay, so what do we do now?"

"We talk to MicroCorp. See if we can find out if they did make those and if so, who they made them for."

Killian wiped the knife and started on a cucumber. "That might not be so easy to do."

I ate a slice of cucumber. "I've got someone working on it."

Teri snorted. "Are you referring to your FBI gal pal?"

I hadn't thought she was listening. "She's not my gal pal."

"Okay," Teri shrugged but her tone said she didn't believe me.

"She's not." I sat on a barstool. I felt tired and my mind spun with ideas, possibilities and theories. None of them seemed to fit anything.

Killian finished the cucumber. "Do you think Micro-Corp will play hardball?"

"Everyone else seems to be."

I WENT to Karen's office. She sat behind her desk. I sat in a chair. Outside, the city basked in sunshine. It was in the nineties today and would be all week.

Karen said, "Tracy identified Senator Hardaway as the Frank that was at the beach house that night."

"Looks like I need to talk to the good Senator again."

"You can't just walk into a Senator's office and accuse him of being at the scene of a murder."

"Sure I can. Especially if he thinks I have something he wants."

"And what would that be?"

"Hardaway wanted to hire me."

Karen raised her brows. "Really?"

"If he wins the White House he told me he'd make me ambassador to Japan."

"Why would he do that?"

"I think it would ensure that I stay out of his hair and quit nosing around in his business," I said. "But that's just a guess."

"Do you think your friend in the Bureau might get something?"

"I don't know. She seems on the up and up. I can't say the same about her partner."

"What if Micro-Corp did make the bugs?"

"Then we can find out who they made them for. It could be one more piece to this puzzle."

Karen shook her head. "I wish I could make sense of all of this."

"I have a theory. Want to hear it?"

"Sure."

"We know a few things. Tracy's father found some-thing that caused him to go to the CIA with it. He got nowhere with them, so he had to find someone else with the resources to help him. I think that was James Forsythe."

"I've talked to several people at his company and no one seems to know anything about what he was working on."

I nodded. "Forsythe was also trying for a deal with MicroCorp. To get it, he'd have to get approval from the Senate Foreign Trade Committee, chaired by Hardaway."

"So what was he doing at the beach house?"

"Sometimes Washington runs best on greased wheels. Maybe Forsythe was trying to give Hardaway a little incentive to pass the deal through."

Karen tapped a pen against her upper lip in thought. "That would make sense. But Forsythe ends up dead."

"True."

"Do you think Hardaway could have killed him?"

"Yes, but I don't think he did," I said. "He's not that stupid."

"You think he's involved?"

"Maybe. Everything is so tangled, who can know?"

"If this was so damn important," Karen said, "Why wouldn't the CIA act on it?"

I chuckled. "You have to understand that the CIA is not the lean mean intelligence machine it's made out to be. It's a cumbersome bureaucracy full of frustrated workers and run by Ivy League snobs who know as much about intelligence work as my cat." I got up. "Time to hit the bricks and snoop some more."

"Be careful."

BY NEXT MORNING, I was in D.C. again. Maybe I should apply for frequent flyer miles.

Whatever faults he might have had, Bill had been a patriot. He loved America, believed in her destiny. He watched from the jungles in Vietnam, then from the halls of the Pentagon, as the CIA fumbled and stumbled in its quest to become the intelligence agency that it could have been, but never achieved. Frustrated with bureaucracies and leadership from Ivy League grads who had never spent one day in the field, Bill had decided to form his own covert ops unit. One not hamstrung by oversight committees and answerable only to a few watchers in the government. One with a low budget that could be snuck into a line item without a peep. It took him ten years but, in the end, he'd done it.

"There'll be no parades, no medals," he said the day he recruited me. "We operate so low under the radar that few people have any knowledge of us."

"So what do we do?" I'd asked.

"We get intelligence on the bad guys," Bill said. "And we use whatever means necessary to protect America."

"Whatever means necessary?"

Bill had nodded and a smiled crossed his face. "Any means."

So it had begun. As I drove past Dupont Circle, I looked up at the plain white building that had been Bill's office. David's office had been moved elsewhere when the unit had downsized. I wondered who was in the old place now.

I checked into a hotel and dialed Hardaway's number. He answered the phone.

"Thought I might come by and have a chat," I said.

"Did you change your mind about working for me?"

"Maybe we need to talk about that."

"Seven o'clock tonight," he said. "I assume you still know where my offices are?"

"I'll be there."

First, I made another stop. I told myself that I wasn't going to do it but some impulse deep inside me needed fed.

It was the kind of thing that I thought addicts who were trying to kick their habit dealt with: that constant tapping on your shoulder, the urge to go and throw yourself into the mire. I wasn't an addict and I wasn't doing anything that would physically harm me. Emotionally, though, I was sure it was going to hurt.

I drove my rental car onto the Beltway and headed for Virginia. The traffic eased as I got farther out and I passed exit signs for places that brought back too many memories. I wanted to turn around but I kept going. Onto a state road that narrowed to two lanes, oak and maple trees in full leaf and brick homes. Dads worked too much, so moms drove their SUV's to soccer matches and attended parent teacher conferences.

Just outside Arlington, I turned into a subdivision and drove two blocks to a two-story home with a double garage. I parked across the street and sat staring at the home. I silently made a bet that the Zen garden would still be in the back. The flowerbed that she'd made was still at the west corner of the porch.

The year since Paris had not dimmed it. Every day went by eased the pain inside but there was still something there that could make me draw a breath at the mention of her name.

Tired of the hollow place in my gut, I drove away, feeling as though I were leaving a piece of me behind.

I EXPECTED him to have a few of his staff around but he was alone. The office was dark except for a desk lamp. Hardaway sat hunched over absorbed in a stack of papers. He looked up when I came in.

"Sit," he said and nodded at the papers. "I've been in the Senate for thirty years and I've never read all the bills that I've voted on." He riffled through the stack. "No one in Washington has the time to read them all." He put the papers aside. "What's on your mind?"

"You were at the beach house the night Forsythe was killed."

"Where did you hear that tale?"

"Tracy identified you from your photo in the paper."

He shook his head. "She's nuts, that girl."

"Nevertheless, Senator, you have a problem."

"Get out of here, Logan."

"What was Forsythe doing? Bribing you to get his takeover deal through? Did he give you Amber and Tracy as a thank you gift?"

"You can't prove a damn thing. You got the word of a United States Senator against a drug-addicted slut. She'd screw a monkey if she could score off of it."

"Personally, Senator, I don't think you killed Forsythe," I said. "Not even you would be that stupid."

"That's the first right thing you've said since you walked in here, son. I didn't kill him."

"What did Bill find that has everyone running scared?"

"Drop it, son. You've no idea what you're snooping into."

"Tell me."

"If I did I'd be as dead as Jimmy-boy."

"What does the elimination of my old unit and Forsythe's death have to do with one another?"

"Let it go, Major."

"I'm not going to let this go and you know it. I want to know why Bill was killed. I want to know why Forsythe was killed and his murder pinned on Bill's daughter."

"Because this is Washington," Hardaway said. "And

powerful people pull very powerful strings." He waved his hand. "My offer still stands."

"No thanks."

He waved me off. "Then I've nothing further to say to you."

I got up. "Okay, Senator, have it your way."

I left. The trip had yielded little so far but it had led me to one thing. Hardaway knew more than he wanted to say and he was scared to say it. The Senator had a reputation for being a tough sort of fellow, hard to bully, and willing to call your bluff. Who was powerful enough to make Hardaway shut his mouth? I didn't have an answer yet.

Keep pulling, John. I could hear Bill's voice in my head. *Keep tugging, pushing, and being a pain in the ass and something will happen.*

My phone rang. It was Healey. "Where are you?"

"D.C."

"What the hell are you doing back up there?"

"Digging. Did you find anything on MicroCorp?"

"They are a legitimate company and are in the running to get bids on some D.O.D. contracts next year. Their technology department is certainly capable of producing the electronics. They have no record of the devices ever being sold to anyone."

"Could they be lying?"

"Maybe but it doesn't get us anywhere. I'd have to prove it. They did report a crate of cargo went missing en route to London a few months ago. The crate contained electronic listening devices. Buyer was a security firm based there. The insurance company paid the bill, the devices were reshipped. Everyone's happy."

"Thanks."

"You owe me one." Healey hung up.

Dusk covered the city and the buzz of street lamps turning on filled my ears as I walked the few blocks to the hotel. I managed to unlock my door and turn on the light before something hard hit me on the head. I don't remember hitting the floor.

19

I WOKE UP IN MY UNDERWEAR, SURROUNDED IN DARKNESS, hands bound behind my back and attached by another rope to my tied ankles. Duct tape covered my mouth; the smell of exhaust was faint in my nostrils. My head throbbed and although I couldn't feel it, I bet there was a nice lump on my skull.

I thought back to the hotel, trying to remember how I ended up in this mess. I'd unlocked the door, turned on the light. I had seen a figure but no detail before I was conked on the noggin.

They teach you that there are certain procedures to follow in situations like this. The first is to ascertain your surroundings. I was in the trunk of a car. A nice car from the condition of the trunk. I wasn't being jostled and the hum of the tires indicated we were on a highway, probably the interstate or the beltway. I heard the occasional pass of a car. There was nothing for me to get my hands on—no tool box, no jumper cables. They'd sanitized the trunk. They weren't amateurs.

The next thing was to test the ropes. They were secure

and the only hope I had was to try to free my hands. Even if I succeeded, it was going to take awhile.

For long moments I flexed, twisted, and tugged, testing the ropes, stretching and maneuvering them to create any amount of space to slip my hands free. After a while, I was no farther along than I was when I'd started. I'd also managed to create a nice cramp in my left shoulder and a rope burn on my left wrist. I felt the car swerve and the sound of the tires changed. We were on a different type of pavement.

I heard air brakes and sounds of diesel engines. We were at a truck stop. Perhaps they were refueling or going to the bathroom. It didn't matter. I could do nothing tied up this way. The night air was hot and humid. Sweat clung to me.

The trunk opened. A powerful flashlight burned into my vision. The person behind it was just a shadow. He reached down and jerked off enough tape for me to talk.

"Still with us?"

"The room service stinks," I said. "And can someone give me a seven o'clock wake-up call?"

He laughed, replaced the tape. The trunk shut and darkness enveloped me again. The light had ruined my night vision.

A few long episodes of flexing and twisting brought me some results. When the trunk had opened, the interior light revealed a small bolt protruding from the trunk lock. I had noted the position and now worked my way over to it. I rubbed against the bolt, wedging it between the rope and my wrist as I rubbed it back and forth. It cut my wrist twice but the blood worked as a lubricant. Painfully, my right hand slid out of the rope.

I started on the other wrist. It was easier and soon the rope loosened. Two more minutes and my legs were free. I was still cramped but I was no longer trussed up like a Christmas turkey.

THE CAR STOPPED. It was cooler now, the humidity gone. No honking of horns, no sounds of traffic. Two car doors slammed then the crunching of footsteps on gravel. The trunk lid opened again.

No flashlight this time, though it was still dark. I'd purposely left the tape over my mouth and had rolled onto my side facing them, posing as though I were still tied up. I needed every second I could get. The figure had a pistol in his left hand and reached down with his right to grab my arm.

"Come on, pal. End of the line—"

It only took a second. My hand came round, grabbed the gun hand, and twisted. Taking the gun away from him, I pulled him in front of me as a shield just in time for him to take two slugs to the gut. He quivered in my grasp.

"Jesus!" I heard somebody say. I gave the dying goon a hard shove and came out of the trunk. The corpse had collided with a second man who brushed his dead friend aside to get a shot at me. I tapped him twice in the chest and he made an oomph noise before dropping to the ground. I grabbed the second man's pistol and rolled into the shadows.

Except for the clearing where the car was parked, there were woods all around me. It was still dark but dawn would come soon. I heard footsteps and swearing.

"Where'd he go?"

"Shit, he took their guns..."

"Watch this guy."

There were three of them. They were within ten feet and didn't see me. I stood behind a tree, watched them, and tried not to shiver. In spite of the cooler air, sweat formed on my brow. Leaves and dirt stuck to me. The ground sloped upward.

One of them kept looking around.

"He could be anywhere—"

"Screw this; I'm getting out of here."

"I'm with you."

The leader was a square-jawed man with the air of a professional soldier. "No one's going anywhere. He's close by."

One of the men was much younger probably no more than early twenties. "He's in his shorts for Christ's sake, barefoot. How far can he go?"

Square-jaw reached out and grabbed the kid by his collar. "This guy is Special Forces trained. You'd better get your head out of your ass or you won't even hear him when he snaps your neck." He glanced around the woods. "Logan, I know you can hear me. We're coming after you. You're not leaving here alive."

They formed a line and headed toward me in an attempt to sweep me into the open. Normally it would be a bad plan to delve into the woods at night searching for a man who knew you were there. But I wasn't exactly up to playing Rambo in the woods. Being barefoot, even small sharp things could cripple me. I didn't know what the terrain was and for all I knew, they could be sweeping me into a secondary team.

Their weakness was that there were only three of them. It was easy for me to flank them and watch their backs as I worked my way back to the car. Just inside the tree line, I studied the vehicle and the cooling bodies of the two men

I'd killed. The car was the best option of escape for me and it would be easy to have a person hiding just out of sight, ready to pick me off if I decided to double back and snatch the car.

It's what I would do.

It took me two minutes but I found him. He was in a small depression a hundred yards from the car, a 30.06 carbine trained on the driver's window. They were betting I'd sneak into the car from the passenger side and slide behind the wheel. Then he'd blow my head off.

He was also a young kid, probably with four or five years of service under his belt before heading into the civilian world to find no work except for hire. It was a tough way to make a living when all you know is how to kill.

By the time he heard me it was too late. My pistol pointed at the back of his head.

"Make a sound and it'll be your last," I said before hitting his head with the butt of the pistol. He slumped down, I threw him over my shoulder, and fireman-carried him to the car. I expected to have to hot-wire it, but the keys were still in the ignition. I gave a solemn thanks to the gods of war. I quickly tied the kid with the ropes that had bound me and stuffed him in the trunk. I found a wallet on the second corpse with three hundred dollars in it. I took it with me. Thirty seconds later, I roared out of there. The sound of the trio shouting, doubtlessly trying to scramble back to the car, echoed through the night. Then a burst of gunfire erupted, but it was too late.

A SIGN TOLD me that I was forty miles to Beckley.

I was in the mountains of southeastern West Virginia.

Some of the state's coalfields were here and the narrow roads wound tight and steep through the mountains. Coal trucks loaded with the black ore passed me on the two-lane roads, making my car vibrate as they passed.

A thump sounded from the rear of the car.

"Hold your horses!" I shouted back. "I can't stop yet!"

More thumping.

"Behave or I'll shoot you now!"

The thumping stopped. I smiled and drove on until I found a small state park that consisted of little more than a rusted barbecue grille and a rotting picnic table. I knew that West Virginia was full of these little parks, neglected for years because of money. The Mountain State was loaded with beauty but it remained startlingly poor. I pulled the car in behind a thick batch of oak trees and opened the trunk.

He was still there, eyes wide. I must have looked like an animal: only in my shorts and covered in leaves, mud, and dirt. I smiled.

"Here's the drill," I said. "I'm getting you out of the trunk. Do what you're told and you'll live. Don't, and I'll kill you. Understood?"

He nodded. He was wiry with a mane of tousled black hair and big teeth. I got him out and loosened the rope so he could finish untying himself. That done, he looked at me.

"Strip."

He didn't want to but he complied and I took his camo pants and t-shirt. I rummaged through the pockets and found a set of handcuffs.

"Is there a key for these?"

"On my keychain."

"Even better," I said. "I'm glad you didn't use these on me." I put him in the front seat and cuffed his hands to the steering wheel. That done, I found a small stream, washed some of the muck off my face, and put on his clothes. They were a little small but they were better than nothing.

I came back to the car. The mountain air was cool; he shivered in his jockey shorts.

"What's your name?"

"Jackson, Scott A."

"Well, Jackson Scott A, you have a problem," I said. "Why were you guys trying to kill me?"

"Aw, hell, mister, I don't know nothing. I just do what Buzz tells me to."

"Buzz," I said. "Who's Buzz?"

"The leader. The guy with the Sgt Rock jaw."

"And who does Buzz work for?"

"We work for Cardigan Security Services."

"Out of D.C.?"

"Baltimore." His teeth were chattering. "I'm cold."

"How long were in the service, Jackson?"

"Three years. Got kicked out for fighting."

"Army?"

"Yeah."

"Give me one reason why I shouldn't ask you some tough questions and snip off body parts when you don't answer me, Jackson."

Real fear surfaced in his eyes. His lower lip shook. "I-I don't know anything..."

"Who owns Cardigan Security?"

"It's owned by some rich guy in Florida. Something Forsythe. To most people we just do regular security, you know. Old men in shopping malls."

"But there's another level?"

He nodded. "Mercenaries, private security, overseas, black ops stuff. Good pay. That's what I wanted to get into."

"You're out of your league," I said.

He dropped his head. "Yeah, I know. But I got a wife."

He had a wedding ring on. I said, "Trying to make the bills, huh?"

A nod. "I was hoping you wouldn't show. I didn't want to have to shoot you."

"You never killed anyone, Jackson?"

"No."

"Take my advice," I said. "Quit Cardigan and go to work in a shopping mall. The pay's not as much but you'll live to celebrate a few more anniversaries with your wife."

"Are you gonna...kill me?"

"No," I said. "Not unless you have something stupid planned." I unlocked the cuffs and tied his hands behind him. I fastened his seat belt. "Sit there and be a good boy."

I pulled out and onto the highway. At dawn we cruised east into Virginia and then into Maryland. I visited an outlet mall, bought some clothes in my size, and gave Jackson's back to him. He put them on gratefully. In a shopping mall outside of Baltimore, I turned to Jackson and unlocked the cuffs.

"Time for you to go," I said. "Get out."

"You're not going to kill me?"

"Are you deaf?"

"No, sir."

"I'm not going to kill you," I said. "Only because of your wife. I see you again under the same circumstances, all deals are off."

He nodded. "Thank you."

"Get lost."

I left him there watching me drive away. Five miles down the road, I ditched the car. I caught the Beltway train into D.C. and an hour later, I walked into the lobby of my hotel. I told the desk clerk I'd lost my key, paid for another one, and found that my room seemed untouched in my absence. I took a hot shower, changed into fresh clothes. That done, I did another security sweep of the hotel and saw no threats. I ordered room service and made a phone call. Teri answered on the third ring.

"How are things in D.C.?"

I told her everything. She listened without interruption until I was done.

"Should you have let the kid go?"

"Seemed like the right thing to do. He was just a kid trying to feed his family. He wasn't up to killing anyone."

"That's a new side of you."

"Maybe."

"No maybe about it," Teri said. "There was a time you'd have gotten all the info he had then killed him."

"That was then."

"You've gotten sentimental."

"Killian says I'm soft."

"Did Shikira have anything to do with it?"

"Let's concentrate on the case, shall we?"

"Okay. Is Karen Lords going to compensate you for all this travel?"

I ignored her. "The Forsythe Group owns the security company that tried to kill me. *Kill.* No normal security firm does that."

"So this kid Jackson said they have another level to the firm. Mercs."

"Yeah. Get Killian to check into the company, see if anything else comes up. Before you leave."

"Leave?"

"I want to search Bill's house and I want you with me."

"Are you forgetting the security men? They're going to be looking for you again."

"I'm not worried about them."

"They kidnapped you, drove you several hundred miles, and almost killed you."

"I can't help that. Without knowing what Bill was working on I'm spinning my wheels."

"I'll be on the next flight out."

"I can only afford a single room on my expense account."

I heard the smile in her voice. "I'll survive."

"Good. I'll meet you at the airport."

"You didn't answer my question. Was Shikira part of the reason you got soft?"

"She was all of the reason," I said. "Get packed."

20

It was a discount motel just off the Beltway, one of dozens in the area. I chose the farthest room from the road they had. The air had been turned off and we walked into a sauna. Teri went over and flicked the A/C on high.

We'd both been in worse. The thin carpet was a dull brown, the walls a subdued tan, and decorated with faded seashells. The bed looked like it would fall apart but Teri sat on it and found it sturdy. The bathroom was clean.

"This will do," I nodded.

"Remember Bratislava?"

I smiled. "Stuck in that roach infested dump for three days. You and the sniper rifle were practically glued together the whole time."

"But I got the shot."

"That you did," I said.

"Did we make a difference, John?" She asked. "I mean, what we did all those times?"

"I don't know," I said. "I left because I didn't think so. I'm not sure how different the world would be now if we hadn't."

"It wasn't the same after you left." Teri put her suitcase on the bed. "Bill wasn't the same, either. He knew the unit he created was gone. It was a matter of time. It wasn't what it used to be."

"And it was my fault."

She shook her head. "No one ever blamed you. You did what you had to do."

"I know. But I can't convince my conscience of it."

She got up and walked behind me; put a hand on my shoulder. "No one blamed you. Not now, not then."

I put my hand atop hers. "Thanks, T."

She smiled. "We're like those forty-seven ronin you once told me about. We had to serve something bigger than ourselves. You still do."

"Not anymore."

"Bull," she said. "This isn't about Tracy. She's a drug addict and if you do get her freed, she'll probably end up in an alley somewhere. We both know it."

"So what is it?"

"It's about your sense of duty to Bill, to the unit, maybe even to the truth."

"Someone's killing off my friends. I want to know who and why."

She reached up and kissed my cheek. "Let's go to Bill's house."

I HADN'T BEEN to Bill's home in over a decade. It was a two-story brick house surrounded by a high wall of thick stone. I knew there was a patio in the rear overlooking a spacious pool.

We snuck over the wall near the rear of the estate. I scanned the area and spotted the small rise. Most of the grass had sprung back up but there were a few telltale blades smashed down.

"This is where the sniper was. I knelt down for a close look.

Teri also knelt and faced the house, trying to get a bead on the line of fire. "He knew where to pick the spot."

We moved toward the house. Water still shimmered in the pool. Beside the patio doors there was a small key panel. I concentrated and tapped a code. The alarm went silent.

"How did you do that?"

"I used to practically live here."

"You'd think a person as well trained as he was in spy craft would have changed the code over the years."

"Man is a creature of habit," I said.

Teri pried the door loose and we went inside. The house smelled musty and old. Being here brought back a lot of memories and for a moment, I was lost in thought.

Teri didn't wait for me to finish reminiscing. She was already moving through the house. She found Bill's study. I joined her a moment later and stood in the doorway.

The study bore the air of pipe tobacco. Mahogany paneling on the walls, thick carpet. There was the familiar oak desk, bare except for a phone. A window behind the desk looked out over the pool.

"The sniper waited until Bill came to the patio doors," Teri said. "How did he know Bill would even do that?"

"What do you mean?"

Teri shrugged. "It's just that if I were going to kill you with a sniper rifle, I would find somewhere that would offer me a good view of the front door. I know you'd come out of the front door eventually. The sniper's position here offered him a good view of the pool area and patio, but it was night.

The chances of Bill coming out there at that hour were slim. I'd have chosen another field of fire."

"I see your point. Seemed like a long shot to think he'd appear at the doors at that hour."

"The FBI said he was talking on the phone when he was shot. Bill did have a habit of walking around when he talked on the phone, especially after the cordless ones came out." Teri's brow furrowed in concentration. "You don't suppose..."

"What?"

"He was talking on the phone and happened not just to walk by the doors, but stand there, right at the perfect spot for the sniper to kill him."

"The sniper called him," I said. "Probably told him to stand there and look out, maybe said 'Look out at the pool, you'll find something interesting'. Something that would make him go to the patio doors."

"No one would do that."

"They would if there was a hint of urgency in the demand...something important."

"The sniper got him to stand exactly where he needed Bill to be in order to shoot him." She slapped her hand on her thigh. "A new twist to the game. An anonymous call to your target and you walk him right into your sights."

I thought it over. "Jesus, Teri, that's thin."

"But it makes sense," she insisted. "John, I can't get past the logic of the sniper's choice of position and timing. If I'm going to shoot someone at night, I'd want to position myself where I expected the most likely chance they'll appear. The position gave you a good view of the patio but it's not the place you'd expect Bill to be at that hour. Unless you talked him into being there."

"And it would have to be someone he knew, someone he'd listen to," I said. I picked up my cell and called Healey.

"Did you guys find out who Bill was talking to the night he was killed?"

"We pulled his phone records, yes."

"So who was he talking to?"

"Agent Barlow worked on that, I think. I'm not sure. Why?"

"I think Bill was set up. I think the killer called him and lured him to stand right at the doors."

"That's a stretch don't you think?"

"Just find out and let me know."

"You're messing in a federal investigation."

"I'll grieve about it later," I said. "Come on, Healey, you aren't getting anywhere as it is. Let me have a nibble and see what I can come up with."

"Let me look at the file and get back with you," she said and hung up.

Teri was already searching the room. "Whatever it was that Bill found...do you think he kept it in here?"

"I can't imagine him keeping it anywhere else."

Teri pulled a clock aside to reveal a safe. The door was slightly ajar. "Looks like the Feds already looked here." She looked inside. "Empty."

"It's obvious that it wasn't in there. The Feds apparently don't have a clue what Bill was working on."

"Would he have taken extra precautions? Another hiding spot?"

"If he knew how volatile the information was, yes he would."

"Maybe he didn't know."

I sat down at the desk. *If I had info to store where would I hide it*?

I let my eyes roam over the study. Pictures adorned the wall to the left of the desk. Memories of a lifetime spent as a soldier and later a spy. There were photos of old friends long gone and of times when saving the world from its evils seemed simpler and honorable. There was Bill receiving the CMH from President Johnson. I smiled at the photo. Bill had hated Johnson, calling him a sneaky, backstabbing oilman.

I looked at the desk. Bill had sat behind it the day he recruited me into his baby, the covert intelligence unit that had been his life's work. The top of the desk was neat and orderly. There was a phone and a pen and pencil set. To the right was a photo of his late wife Elisa and Bill in younger times. On the left side was a photo that made me stop.

It showed Bill, me, Teri, and several other members of our unit. I remembered the clearing, the smell of the jungle around us and the feeling of euphoria that we'd had. Another trip into Hell was done and we'd lived to tell the tale. Each face in the photo brought back memories.

"*You can count on nothing in this world, John-o,*" Bill once told me. "*I'm sure your parents and your uncle loved you beyond words, but we are mortal and every-thing in this life passes away. You are the only one that you can depend on.*"

I reached for the right side drawer and pulled it out. A few miscellaneous items were inside. Pencils, pens, paper clips. Rubber bands, scissors. A four-by-six framed photo of Mozart buried beneath it all....

"Teri," I said.

She was on her knees, running her hands along the floor molding.

I took the photo out. "This is odd."

She looked up and I showed her the picture.

"That's strange," she said. "Bill hated classical music."

"So why would he have this photo of Mozart?"

I examined the photo. Nothing special, apparently copied from an encyclopedia or printed from the Web. I flipped the frame over and loosened the tiny fasteners that held the backing in place. Teri forgot her examination and watched intently. The pins removed, I slid the cardboard back out of the frame.

"There's something in here," I said. "Behind Mozart."

It was a tiny micro SD card.

Teri inserted it into her phone. "It's encrypted."

"Can you decode it?"

She shrugged.

21

Special Agent Healey looked across the bay. "So, what did you guys do in the spy game?"

Two days back from Baltimore, I was on the foredeck watching the sunlight shimmer over the bay. The water was a deep blue-green on this late afternoon.

"That, I'm afraid, is classified."

"Don't mess with me, Logan," she said. "All FBI agents carry high level clearances."

"And it wouldn't have gotten you past the door in my old unit," I said. "Uncle Sam made me sign an agreement. I could be jailed for telling you anything."

"I'll guarantee the Bureau doesn't press any charges, given the circumstances."

"Another thing," I said. "I don't trust your partner."

"I'm sorry you feel that way."

"Who was Bill talking to on the phone?"

She sighed. "That's classified."

"You want my help without giving me any info I can use to help you."

"What do you want from me, Logan? I'm trying to solve a

case here. Every turn, every clue I get, it's buried. Every attempt I make gets undermined. I don't know who to trust."

"And the detail of who Bill was talking to the night he died is missing."

Healey couldn't look at me. "Yes."

"Who could be sabotaging the investigation?"

"The Bureau, my...partner..." she let out a breath. "Everybody."

"Walk away from it," I said. "Let the Bureau do its thing. I'll have to do this on my own."

"I can't let you do that. Would you let it go if you were me?"

"No," I said.

She gave me that same look women use when men have just proven them right.

"Who was Bill talking to?"

Healey rolled her eyes. "Dammit, I don't know. The file, according to my superiors, is in the hands of the upper level agents."

"Isn't that unusual?"

"Very."

"Did you bring that up?"

"I did," she said. "Do you have some liquor around here?"

"Crown?"

"That will do. On ice."

I brought her the drink and she took a pull. She said, "My partner, Agent Barlow, complained to the SAC. I was told to drop this case and move on. Forsythe had some powerful strings, Logan, but someone else has even more. I've been put on paid leave for three weeks."

"Then it's just you and me."

She looked up. "I'm not sure I can trust you."

"Good, I don't trust you, either."

"What made you leave the spy game?"

"Six years ago, my team had an assignment to track down a former Soviet KGB general Leonid Grinkov. Grinkov, like most KGB officers, found himself in uncertain territory upon the breakup of his nation. Gorbachev had signed the order effectively eliminating the KGB as it stood and Grinkov not only had a wife, but a mistress in Kiev that had very expensive tastes."

"Many of them do."

I nodded. "Grinkov began selling arms on the black market. The Soviet system had collapsed and inventory controls and accountability were non-existent. From arms he moved up to bigger toys—tanks, missiles, helicopters."

"What about nukes? Seems the Soviets don't have a complete listing."

"We'd heard rumors that Grinkov was shopping around for a legitimate buyer for a low-grade nuke. He supposedly found one. We tracked him to Chile; an estate just outside a hole in the wall village. I put my team in place for surveillance. We wanted to identify the buyer. We waited, but they knew. It was an ambush. Only Gina and I made it out alive."

"Did you get the nuke?"

"Never showed up. We never found the leak."

Healey shook her head. "I don't follow. Why would Bill be concerned?"

"It haunted Bill, the fact that some insider could have set his team up, that someone might be a traitor. Our team was a ghost. It didn't exist on any record.

"It had to be someone from the inside."

I nodded. "The whole incident would eventually lead to Bill's retirement. For me, it was another reminder of how screwed up the whole thing had become. I decided to get out. I had my wife and wanted to be with her."

"You got disillusioned."

"Yes," I said. "I guess I did."

She slumped in the chair. "I got into this job because I believed the Bureau stood for truth and justice. I wanted to help make a difference."

"Have you?"

"Sometimes I think so. Other times I have to wonder."

"What about now?"

She smiled. "To be honest, I have no idea."

"I know the feeling."

"It's all politics now. The agents bust their asses and the management overrides them."

"It sounds like nothing has changed."

She got up. "I'm going to go to the beach and drink myself blind the next two days."

"Sounds like a plan."

She put the drink down. "What about you?"

"Going to try and connect the dots."

She laughed. "You never give up do you?"

"No."

"Were you always this tenacious?"

"I tried to be."

"Then I'm glad you were on our side."

A few minutes later Healey left. I sat for a long time watching the water. My left hand dangled down and I gently rubbed Lucky. If I closed my eyes, I could still see the village and feel the heat that made the air shimmer. The dust rose from the street when you walked. I could picture Grinkov as I saw him through my binoculars. The café at the end of the street. Grinkov sat at a table dressed in a white suit. My team was in place and everything seemed normal.

Then Grinkov looked up, straight at me and smiled. He knew I was there.

Voices in my ear. My team, reporting enemy approaches. Sounds of gunfire and suddenly bullets whizzed around me.

Teri had not been with me there. Gina Kennedy, the woman who had died in L.A. had been. Only she and I had lived to fight another day. Now she was dead and I couldn't help but think that I had risked my life to save her only to have it taken away. In the end, I hadn't saved her, just prolonged her death.

But wasn't it all we ever did? We clung to life, fought for it tenaciously, all the while knowing it was futile. Death claims us all when it's all said and done and there was nothing I could do about it.

東

Killian showed up an hour later. He grabbed a beer before meeting me on the top deck.

"Benson Hilliard is CEO of Cardigan Security Services." Killian dropped the file onto my lap. "Forsythe is a partner, helped Hilliard with the startup costs."

"What else?"

"They do everything from security guards in shopping malls to security in Iraq and Afghanistan. Two of their employees were tried for murder in Afghanistan but were acquitted."

"What about Hilliard?"

"According to his bio, a born-again Christian who believes that God has a destiny for America and it is his duty as a follower to help fulfill that destiny."

"By doing what?"

"By doing whatever it takes to keep America safe."

“So, we have Forsythe who owns a piece of Cardigan. Someone uses them to try to kill me. Forsythe also tried to buy MicroCorp and someone uses them to bug my boat.”

“And we know it can’t be Forsythe so that eliminates one suspect from our list.” Killian finished his beer and set the bottle beside him. “Being dead has its advantages in this case.”

I leaned back and thought for a while. “I’m going to talk to Emily Forsythe again.”

22

"I APPRECIATE YOU LETTING ME HAVE ACCESS, MRS. Forsythe," I said. "I promise I'll try to hurry as much as I can."

"Emily," she said. She was in a light green minidress and high heels. Her eyes raked over Killian again but ignored Teri. "And you're welcome, although I don't know what you expect to find. Jim only took *The Golden Egg* out when he had a big party going on and wanted privacy."

Dana Costello had mentioned Forsythe's yacht. Rumors swirled about the activities that had happened through the years on the boat. I didn't know if we'd find anything of importance on the yacht but I was running out of places to look.

"Have the authorities looked at the yacht at all?"

"They gave it a cursory examination, I think. Nothing much."

"We'll try to be quick."

"Please let me know if you need anything," she said.

"Before you go…" I pulled out a picture and handed it to her. "Do you recognize this man?"

She studied the photo, shook her head and handed it back. "He looks familiar. Maybe he was at one of our parties. Between those and my charity work I can't always remember everyone."

"You ever heard of a man named Benson Hilliard?"

"Of course. He's a dear friend of the family. He gave a hundred grand for my orphanage in Haiti last year."

"What do you know about his company, Cardigan Security?"

She gave me an apologetic smile. "Nothing, I'm afraid. I know that James owned part of it. He helped Benson get it off the ground. He's done a fine job with it. Ben, I mean."

"If you remember anything else, I'd appreciate you letting me know."

"Sure." Emily Forsythe gave me another smile, this one full of promises before walking down the dock, her rear doing battle with the minidress.

Teri snorted. "The grieving widow."

Killian said nothing but the corners of his mouth twitched. We stood for a moment staring at The Golden Egg. I'd done some research on it. A hundred and twenty-five feet in length, and rising five decks high above the water line, it boasted a helicopter landing pad, full size pool with faux rock grotto, and gold faucets.

We walked on board and Teri whistled. "Wonder how much this baby costs to operate?"

"More than we all make in a year," I said.

Teri ran her hands across the polished brass railing. "Okay, boss, where do we start?"

"Office, staterooms, anywhere that might have a safe or hiding places," I said. "Maybe Forsythe left something on here showing what the hell he was doing mixed up in all of this. Did you bring your safe cracking tools?"

Killian held up a bag. "Never leave home without them."

"Good," I said. "This could be a big waste of everyone's time, but better safe than sorry."

We started with Forsythe's stateroom. Rich paneling and a mirrored ceiling provided the décor. Teri checked the bed, the mattress, box springs, looked under it and checked the railings themselves, in case someone had hidden something along the grooves. Killian looked for the safe in the walls and floor. I went through the dresser and closet. I checked under the drawers and dug through the clothing to check the bottom.

We came up with nothing. So we headed to his office.

The office that Forsythe worked from was a smaller room off the stateroom. It had a desk, bookcase, and two leather chairs. A TV hung from the ceiling in the corner. On the desk was a computer. It showed a wireless internet connection.

"Let's see what Forsythe was into online," Teri said and started tapping at the keys.

Killian and I went through the routine again. We checked the desk and the adjacent bookcase and came up empty.

"This is interesting," Teri said.

"How'd you get into his computer and can't crack Bill's decryption code?"

"Because it's an advanced algorithm and without the key it will take time," Teri replied. "Forsythe takes his yacht to Aruba twice a year."

"Why is that interesting? He could afford it."

"But check this out..." Teri motioned us over. "I brought up a GPS program. You can plot the route you want to take somewhere and plot it into the ship's navigation. This one is for his bi-yearly run to Aruba. See here?"

Killian nodded. "It avoids all the ports and major shipping lanes."

"Does he take the covert route every time?"

"Looks like it."

"Now why would he do that unless he didn't want anyone to know he was there?"

"He wouldn't," I answered. "When was his last trip?"

"Six weeks ago," Teri answered.

Tracy was with Forsythe at that time. I made a note to talk to her about it. I glanced at Killian. He was thinking the same thing that I was and gave me a miniscule nod.

"On it," he said and disappeared from the office.

Teri stared at the screen. "Are you thinking what I'm thinking?"

"Yes, but let's wait until Killian confirms it. Can you take the hard drive with you and tap into it further?"

Teri looked at me.

"Sorry," I said. "Of course you can."

Teri continued to tap at the keys. "Thank you for recognizing my genius."

She continued tapping on the keyboard without finding anything else. Killian appeared in the doorway. "You better come take a look."

THE NEXT MORNING, Karen stood at the window of her office looking at the city skyline. "You have got to be kidding me."

I took a sip of coffee. "Do you have another explanation for it?"

She turned around and gave me that look that made witnesses sweat. "You're telling me that James Forsythe, the richest man in the state, has a false bottom on his million dollar yacht and goes to Aruba twice a year using a route that avoids all contact with authorities?"

"That's what I'm saying."

"And why would he do that?"

"You tell me; you're the one with the Harvard Law degree."

"Smuggling."

"Certainly looks that way, doesn't it?"

"But what? Drugs?"

"I don't know. Weapons perhaps. Forsythe was a patriot."

Karen said, "Aruba's also known for white slavery."

I merely nodded.

Karen looked back out the window. "Why would Forsythe need to smuggle anything? Why would he need to be involved in something like that? That's just plain stupid."

"Want to go on the yacht with me? I'll show you the false hull and the route he used, all laid out with GPS precision."

"That's thin, but it might explain his murder."

"Pieces are coming together, Karen. Slowly but surely."

"If you can establish a little more proof in that, it might be the reasonable doubt that I need to get Tracy off the hook."

"I think there's more to it than that."

"You think your friend was involved?"

"Bill would never get mixed up in this," I said. "But he knew Forsythe."

"But how did they know each other?"

"I have an appointment with someone who might tell me."

WE MET at an outside café a block from the bay. The

lunchtime traffic noise combined with the patrons around us would make it hard for someone to use a mike on us.

"I hope you appreciate me driving all the way up here."

"I do, Carl, I really do. How's the nightclub?"

He made a derisive snort. "Got a visit from Langley. Told me to stay away from you. I told them you came to me and I didn't have much choice."

"But yet you came."

"Maybe I'm tired of doing something just because they tell me to," Carl said, taking a bite of his crab salad. "This is good."

"Talk to me."

"One: Bill Rochelle and Forsythe met in the mid eighties. Forsythe's company was just starting and Forsythe was looking to invest in companies with big defense contracts. He had his sights set on a small company who, rumor had it, had developed a new computer processor that could help the navigation systems on fighter jets. Forsythe went to Washington to talk to some Pentagon brass about it."

"And he met Bill?"

"Purely by accident," Carl said. "Some sort of fund-raiser thing. Anyway, whatever his faults, Forsythe knew opportunities when he saw them. He got wind of Bill's covert unit and Forsythe was a patriot. Over the years, he used his own company's resources to help you guys out whenever he could."

"What resources?"

"Whatever he could. Money, equipment. Forsythe could ship anything anywhere. He had the means and money to do it. Bill had planned the assassination of a top Libyan general. I believe you might recall that particular one."

"I don't know what you're talking about."

"Of course," Carl said. "Anyway, the team snuck into

Libya on a freighter from Malta across the Med and to a small village on the coast called Silt. That freighter belonged to a shipping company owned mostly by Forsythe Investment Group. After the job was done, the shipping company got a new contract with a Libyan exporter and the CIA got a new way to keep tabs on the country."

"I'm surprised Qadhafi would have approved that."

"Easy. Your unit—I mean the unit that went in—planted false evidence that the general was planning a coup. Qadhafi was glad to see him go."

"What else?"

"Word is Forsythe got caught up in the excitement. He found the day-to-day operations of running a company boring. He started branching out."

"Into what?"

"More exciting stuff. Word has it he was bringing it in twice a year on his yacht."

"Weapons?"

Carl looked around and nodded. "Heroin."

"Hard to believe a guy with Forsythe's money would do something so stupid."

"That's the word I'm hearing. Forsythe's company had dealings with the world, Logan. He had ships all over, planes, trucks. He picked it up in the Golden Crescent region in Afghanistan and shipped it to a holding company in Aruba. They're not sure yet how he got it out through their ports."

"He didn't. He had the carrier ship drop it off before it made port and he picked it up in his yacht. Forsythe made two trips a year to Aruba on his yacht. There's a nice false hull on it. He also had a route that skirted the shipping lanes and avoided the local authorities."

"Guess that cost him a pretty penny," Carl said. "But

then the law in the Caribbean can be bought pretty cheaply."

"That's true."

"Word also says that Forsythe's money came mostly from this stuff. Apparently his business dealings weren't all they were cracked up to be."

"Still hard to believe."

"One more thing. Forsythe made a call to Rochelle a day before he died."

"Does Langley know why?"

"No. Just guesses. And Langley's guesses are never any damn good." Carl finished the salad. "I didn't realize how big this city is," he said. "Maybe I can branch out, open a club here."

"Do me a favor and stay in Miami. I have enough problems with government people here as it is."

23

Jake Ross' office was a glass cubicle situated in the corner of the squad room. It was neat and organized. Framed photos of what I assumed to be family sat on the right side of his desk. He leaned back, put his feet up on the desk, took a sip of coffee from an oversized mug, and stared at the ceiling.

"Those are some crazy theories you're spouting."

"I found the false hull, the navigation charts, and I have an associate digging further into Forsythe's re-cords."

"Go to the Bureau and tell them."

"I don't quite trust them. They half-assed this case, Jake, you and I both know that. They should have gone through Forsythe's finances, checked his hard drives, spoken to company people. They barely touched any of it."

"Someone wants this case to go away fast. That's not exactly news." Ross put his feet down and leaned for-ward. "So why are you telling me?"

"Because you're the only cop I trust."

"Jesus, Logan, you're putting me in a hell of a spot."

"I know."

Ross looked at the ceiling again. "Can you imagine if I were to call the press and say that Forsythe was running drugs? They'd have my badge two minutes later."

"Question is where did it go once it got here? He had to hand it off to someone."

"Someone in his organization?"

"It would make the most sense. Wouldn't you try to do it that way?"

"I suppose I could check with Greg over in Narcotics. Maybe he has a C.I. who might know something. That's Confidential Informant, by the way." Ross grinned.

"I know what it is."

The grin vanished. "Let me see what I can do. After all, it's not as if I'm officially opening up the investigation or sticking my nose in it. Just simple human curiosity, right?"

"Of course."

I called Teri. She was still working to crack the code. I told her to hurry up. She told me something that wasn't very nice and hung up.

TRACY DENIED KNOWING anything about Forsythe running drugs. She admitted that they did go to Aruba and that Forsythe kept parts of the trip a secret from her. The date on Forsythe's computer matched when Tracy relayed they'd last made a trip there.

"Did Jim tell you why?"

"He never said, really. Just said it was for the hell of it and brushed it away."

"Do you know of any cargo coming on board?"

"Look, samurai, one of the things you learn about having a sugar daddy is you don't ask a lot of questions that might derail the gravy train, you understand what I'm saying? Jim treated me good—better than any other guy—so I didn't bother nosing around in his business."

I returned from the jail to my boat, sat on the deck, drank a beer, and watched the water.

Teri showed up carrying a gym bag. "Ready?"

"For what?"

"You were supposed to take me to the dojo."

"You're supposed to be working on that encryption code."

"The computer is doing it."

"Maybe later."

She cocked her head at me, raised her eyebrows. "All right. We'll do it the hard way."

She went inside and came out in sweats and a tee.

"Let's go, tough guy."

"You mean here on the boat?"

"You had your chance of a nice dojo floor; now you have to settle for your boat."

"We'll spar later."

"No," she said. "I have to kick your ass now."

I barely got to my feet before she launched a series of kicks and rapid-fire arm strikes. Teri hadn't lost her sharpness in the years and I'd almost forgotten how good she was. We worked our way inside where she granted me a second to clear a space in the living room before she came at me. I blocked a roundhouse kick and she swept my feet, putting me hard on my back. Twisting left, right, to avoid her stomping my face in, I grabbed her ankle and flipped her. As I came to my feet, she tried a punch. I trapped her arm. She used her free arm to try another. I grabbed it, too, and now held both wrists. We were close, our bodies almost touching. Her breath was warm on my cheek.

"You're still sharp," I said.

"You have no idea." Our mouths met in a kiss that brought back memories of a lifetime before. The kiss grew more passionate until there was no turning back for either of us.

Afterward, lying in bed with her arm across my chest and my nose in her hair, I had to wonder if I was doing the right thing.

"Do you think the deaths of the team and Forsythe's murder really has something to do with Shikira's death?" Teri asked.

I held her close. I didn't want to think about it.

DETECTIVE GREG HUMPHREYS had long dirty black hair and a scruffy beard. His jeans were torn and grungy, and Jimi Hendrix's bandana-wearing head plastered the front of his tee shirt. He sat down with an apologetic look at Ross. "Sorry I'm late, Lieutenant."

We were alone in a bar on the south side of the harbor. The jukebox cranked out Guns N'Roses and we sat in a corner booth where we could watch the door.

"It's okay," Ross said. "What do you have?"

"I had a snitch who has a small boat. Got it from his dad or something. Anyway, he tells me he used to get paid five hundred bucks for going out just beyond the harbor and picking up a package. Said it was always dropped off of a yacht out there. He had instructions to take it to an insurance company over on Riverdale. Put it in the mail slot."

Ross said, "Can we talk to this guy?"

"No can do. I told him I wanted details on the operation. He was supposed to get me the name of the yacht, but the night of the meet, he ended up in an alley off Caderas. He'd been beaten to death. From the type of bruises and the force of impact, M.E. said the killer probably knew martial arts."

"Any witnesses?"

"One person said they saw what looked like a Chinese guy walking near the vicinity around that time."

"Who is this witness?"

Humphreys tamped out his cigarette. "Dead two days later. Mugging."

"Pretty coincidental," Ross retorted.

"Tell me about it.

東

"AHA," Teri said tapping at the keyboard. "Gotcha."

"What did you get?" I looked over her shoulder at the screen.

"A nice list of companies. Something tells me that they're not all on the books."

"That isn't Bill's stuff."

"It's Forsythe's hard drive. He has some nice encryption on here. What do you think I've been working on all of this time?"

"Bill's chip."

"John, that baby is top of the line encoded. I may have to go to some sources I know for a high-tech program."

"Keep it low key." I studied the computer screen. "There's an insurance company in Riverdale. The guy in Narcotics said that they did drop-off's there."

"Still no smoking gun though."

"Keep snooping," I said. "Maybe you'll get lucky."

Her gaze fixed onto the screen. "Any regrets?"

"Not really. Brought back some good memories. What about you?"

"No."

"Good. Now if you would do me a favor and dig up everything you can on that insurance company, I'd be grateful."

"How grateful?"

"Oh, very."

She smiled. "I love a grateful man." She poured through the files. Then, "Holy Mother of God."

"What?"

"I think I just found the decryption software for Bill's chip."

24

The next morning found me sitting across the street from a single-story brick office building located on a corner lot. The sign said DEVONSHIRE INSURANCE COMPANY. The parking lot had spaces for ten cars but a brown sedan was its only occupant. Over the next two hours, people came and went. I didn't recognize any of them. There was a sign by the door that said AFTER HOURS DROPOFFS and an arrow pointing to a slot in the wall. It was a large slot, easily big enough for a package. This would be where Humphrey's snitch would have dropped off the dope.

I thought about going in and decided against it. I would find nothing out. It also might tip them off. Forsythe's companies seemed pretty well interlinked. If I were on anyone's target list within the Forsythe Group, I would bet that everyone would know me.

A Mercedes-Benz sedan rolled down the street and pulled into the parking lot. I watched Emily Forsythe get out and walk inside. My phone rang.

"Where are you?" Teri asked.

"Still staking out Devonshire."

"Well I staked them out online. They handle all the insurance needs for the Forsythe Group. Forsythe had a life insurance policy on him through Devonshire."

"How much?"

"Ten million."

"I just saw the widow go into the office."

Teri gave a snort of derision. "Maybe she's there to collect."

TWO HOURS LATER, I was in Karen's office.

"I've had an accountant examine Forsythe's books," Karen reached across her desk and handed me a report. "There were some...irregularities."

I glanced at the paper. "How?"

"The Forsythe Group itself seems perfectly above board," Karen said. "No accounting errors, everything is okay there. But Forsythe seems to have had some side projects he was working on. And those are the problem. It wasn't easy to track. This stuff was hidden under a lot of layers, but my accounting firm is the best. They found them."

"Such as?"

"Forsythe showed personal income that doesn't quite go back to a legitimate revenue source. My girl found some companies that seem to exist only on paper, a bank account in the Bahamas, and an office suite in Miami for an import company with no employees working there."

"Good set up to launder money," I said.

"I couldn't keep this under wraps. I took it to the State Attorney. They're going to drop charges against Tracy."

"That quickly?"

"With all of this information coming to light it will be easy for me to show reasonable doubt to a jury. They didn't have much to begin with and this revelation just weakens their case even further." She reached into her desk drawer and handed me a check. "This is for a job well done."

It was a nice check. I got up and stuck out my hand. "Call me if you need me."

She got up and walked around the desk. She stuck out her hand. "Don't worry, I will."

KILLIAN WAS DRIVING a silver Saab convertible. We took the Jackson Street entrance to the freeway. You didn't seem to ride in this car, you floated.

"Where'd you get this baby?"

"Got it from a guy in Miami who no longer needed it."

"You're a persuasive fellow."

"My good looks and charm. What's up with her release?"

"With the revelation of Forsythe's side business, I think the possibility that someone else could have pulled the trigger increased. I think the state decided to cut their losses and avoid taking Karen on in court. She can be pretty ruthless."

"I've heard."

We parked at the jail and stood by the car. We didn't need to wait long.

Karen accompanied a healthy looking Tracy Rochelle out of the county jail to the sight of a dozen reporters shoving microphones and cameras at them.

"—what do you have to say to the DA now that you're free?"

"—is this some kind of bargain?"

"—Ms. Rochelle, how do you feel now that you've been cleared?"

Killian said, "So that's Bill's girl."

"Yeah."

"Pretty."

"Uh-huh."

Karen faced the cameras. Tracy stood behind her, looking shocked and shy.

"I just want to say that justice still works here in America and I want to thank the State Attorney's office for realizing that there was no evidence to link my client to this horrible crime. I'm sure that they will exhaust every avenue to find the true killer. For now, my client wishes to be alone for a while and to recover from the death of her father and from this tragic and traumatic event. Our thoughts and prayers go out to the Forsythe family over their loss and I'm confidant that justice will be done."

More questions were shouted but Karen pushed her way through with the ferocity of a linebacker. She spotted Killian and I and motioned us over.

"What are you doing here?"

"Moral support," I said. "This is Mason Killian. He's an associate."

"Are you a PI, too?"

"I've watched *Barnaby Jones* a few times," Killian said without cracking a smile.

Karen looked at me. "Same smart-ass mouth, I see. Twins?"

"I'm the better looking one," Killian said.

I gestured at Tracy. "Where is she going now?"

"She's staying with me for a few days until we get the details of her father's estate done. I think she's entitled to some of it now that she's free. She also has to finish counseling."

"Okay." I walked over to Karen's Mercedes where Tracy stood leaning up against the fender. "Hey, kid. Congratulations."

"Thanks." She looked down at the ground then back up at me. "I guess I need to thank you. For everything."

"You're welcome. Just stay clean and sober. That will be plenty thanks enough."

She smiled, put her arms around my neck, and hugged me. I held her and for a moment, I had a heavy feeling that this was a temporary respite, that dark forces were gathering and I wanted at that moment to whisk Bill's daughter out of there and take her somewhere safe and secluded.

"Why don't you come and stay with me for a few days?"

"Thanks, samurai, but I'll be fine."

"You might be safer with me."

"It's over," she said. "I'm off the hook."

"Where will you go?"

"I'm going to stay with Karen for a few days until I get things figured out."

"You could stay with me."

"Thanks, samurai, but I think Karen would be better for me right now."

"Okay. If you need me, you have my number, right?"

"Yeah," she said.

We broke the embrace and I watched her get into the car with Karen. I gave a silent prayer for Bill to watch over his daughter.

"Why don't I feel good about this?" I asked Killian.

He didn't answer, just kept those sunglasses trained on the car growing smaller in the distance.

25

Emily Forsythe met me in the same room where I'd first made her acquaintance. She wore designer jeans and a red colored tank top. She was barefoot and I noticed an ankle bracelet on her left leg. She hadn't been drinking this time. She shook my hand and offered me a seat.

"You've been a busy man."

"I try."

"What have you found out?"

"Did you know James was smuggling heroin in the false bottom of his yacht?"

She wrinkled her face, as though trying to stifle a laugh. "What are you talking about?"

"We looked at the yacht, Emily. There's a false hull on the boat. His computer showed he made covert trips to Aruba twice a year."

"I'm afraid I don't know anything about that."

"Have you ever gone to Aruba on the yacht with him?"

"Of course."

"Know anything about the route he took?"

"I never paid any notice. James always handled that."

"You didn't notice anything unusual? Unexplained stops? Strange people on board?"

"I'm afraid not. But it's a big boat."

"Did he dock anywhere?"

"Sometimes. He also liked to cruise along the north side of the island. There was a secluded beach that I liked." She smiled. "I like being naked on the beach. Maybe we could go together sometime."

Secluded. It could make a nice place to pick up stuff unseen.

"He made a trip six weeks before he died. Tracy was with him."

She bit her bottom lip and closed her eyes. "He told me he was going to Key West to look at some investment property."

"Why didn't you go?"

"I had a board meeting for one of my charities that week."

"We also have it on good authority that a man was paid to go out into the bay and pick up drugs that were thrown off the yacht and take it to the Devonshire offices."

I could see the wheels turning in her brain. Emily Forsythe wasn't stupid. She was thinking things through. If she took over her husband's company it would be in good hands.

"How did he avoid customs?"

"He took a route that avoided a lot of local law enforcement in the area. Moreover, he got rid of the drugs before coming into the harbors. And I'm sure you're a smart enough woman to realize that Caribbean police are notoriously corrupt."

She sighed. "You know, I was angry that no one seemed to be digging into my husband's death. Now I wish they hadn't. That you hadn't."

"The police will be talking with you, Emily. Your hands may be clean but they don't know that."

"I swear I didn't know anything about his dealings. I told you that from the start."

"The feds are not so easily convinced."

She put her face in her hands, mumbling, "Jesus, Jim, what were you doing?"

"There's something else. Men from Benson Hilliard's security company kidnapped me and tried to kill me."

She raised her head. "Why would Benny want to kill you?"

"I've been asking myself that question," I answered. "Your businesses appear to be fully intertwined with each other in many ways. Perhaps someone from inside the company is pulling some nasty strings."

Her eyes widened. "You're not meaning me?"

"It's a logical leap, Emily."

"Mr. Logan, I swear..." She reached over and took my hand. "John...I swear—"

"So we're on a first name basis?"

"I didn't order anyone to kill you. I'm not in charge of Jim's company. The Board of Directors has to make that vote and that won't happen until next week. Right now, I own most of it, but I don't run it."

"Then who else could be?"

"I don't know."

"Which leads back to you."

"I don't know how else I can convince you. I gave them the company's books. That should prove some-thing."

"It does. Your husband had a lot of dummy companies set up."

She looked at me and for the first time I saw tears in her eyes. "I'm going to lose my husband's company, aren't I?"

I couldn't answer her. I didn't know.

I WENT HOME. It was done. My obligation, my *giri* had been fulfilled. Tracy was free and Karen had paid me handsomely for the job. But it wasn't over. Eventually this thing would play out. All their attempts to kill me had failed so far. Sometimes it was skill but not always. Despite years of training and practice, sometimes survival came down to pure luck. I spent the day on household chores and sitting with Lucky in my lap watching the water. I went to bed but I couldn't sleep. The events of the past weeks kept turning over in my head. Everything was jumbled and disconnected. It would take some more digging to link it all together.

My phone rang.

"I have it," Teri said on the other end.

She told me what she'd found. I listened, unwilling to believe what she was telling me. I hung up the phone feeling sickened and angry. But I had no time to mourn.

I heard Lucky meow and the boat gave a slight tip. Someone had just stepped onboard.

All of the drapes were shut and the interior drowned in black so my eyes were already adjusted to the darkness. I slipped out into the living room. My *daisho*--the twin swords given to me by Funichi when I left Japan—sat on a low teakwood table. I eased the longer one—the katana—from its scabbard. I stepped back into the shadows and waited.

It was another five minutes before they moved, approaching from both fore and aft doors. Since you can't be in both places at once you handle the nearest threat first. It came from the front door, a muted cough of a silenced pistol and the lock shattered. The shadow came into the room and I stepped out. He turned, the pistol coming up to bear—

I came from the shadows. *Hasuji otosu*, the straight cut, sliced across his belly, opening him up like a ripe melon. He fell, but I was already moving, bare feet silent on the floor heading toward the aft part of the houseboat. My combat instinct was in full gear, senses sharpened and alert, aware of everything around me. Dawn was an hour away, the first hint of sunlight glowing red on the horizon. The bay was still inky black and calm. The houseboat rocked gently and I saw the second man barge in. The door had nearly been taken off its hinges; he came though, and I simply plunged the blade into him and withdrew it in one fluid motion, just as Funichi had taught me so long ago. I moved straight through and onto the deck as movement came to my right.

I spun, blade out and horizontal, crouching low and avoiding the elbow strike that could have taken my head. My blade cut him at the knees and he screamed but I cut the cry short with an upward strike that sliced him open from crotch to neck.

Back inside, the stench of death invaded my nostrils. I stopped and listened. In the distance gulls cried and the diesel engines of a tugboat sounded across the night water.

I searched the bodies. Silenced Berettas, Marine fighting knives, no ID, one set of car keys with an alarm fob. None of the faces meant anything to me. I moved out to the parking lot. A black Ford Explorer that didn't belong to anyone who lived here sat in a parking slot. I hit the button on the fob and the car beeped. The engine was still ticking and I touched the hood. Warm.

I searched inside. There was a bag of empty fast food wrappers, and a half empty soda can. The rental agreement was in the glove box and there was a motel key in the change holder.

I went back to the boat and called Killian.

"Yo." He sounded awake. I wondered if he ever slept.

"Did I wake you?"

"No."

"I got three stiffs at my boat. Sneaking on board, real commando stuff. I need a clean up. Their SUV's in the parking lot. Can you make them disappear?"

"Sure. But you don't want to call the cops?"

"No. I want them to vanish. See if we can spook the enemy a little."

"I'm on it. Where are you going?"

"I'm going to check out their room."

Killian grunted and hung up.

THE HOTEL WAS an inexpensive chain near the freeway for the travelers and executives who needed a simple place to crash for the night. There was nothing exclusive about it; it could be a hotel in a million different towns. The room was at the far end of the parking lot. I stood at the door and listened. There was no sound from inside and I knocked. Still no answer. I unlocked the door and went in.

There were two beds; suitcases sat on both of them. I snapped on some latex gloves, opened the suitcases, and rummaged through clothing and underwear. There were British passports and the faces matched the men who lay dead on my boat. Edward Long, John Adams, and Lyle Edwards. I didn't think the names were real. Long was the one I'd taken first. They also had photo I.D. cards from Cardigan Security Services. I finished my search and found nothing else. Disappointed, I took the passports and went back home. On the way I called Ross.

The SUV and the bodies were gone by the time I got back. There was no trace of blood. Killian must have had help. I didn't ask.

I sat looking at the passports. They looked real yet they didn't and I couldn't decide. I decided to do some-thing else and started to fix my door.

Killian appeared.

"Couldn't help but notice you'd played Samurai Jack with those three."

"I wanted to use profanity but it didn't seem to work as well."

Killian nodded. "Gotta go with what works." He grabbed a hammer and, in a minute, I heard him working on the other door. When we finished the sun was high in the sky and I was starving. Killian made breakfast. He brought the eggs, bacon, and toast outside, and we ate on the deck.

"A real breakfast," I said. "Just like in Texas."

"Except everything's bigger."

"Everything?"

Killian nodded. "Everything."

"The wonder trio had British passports," I said. "Names sound kind of phony. They also worked for Cardigan. Otherwise their room was clean."

"So what did you do?"

"I called Ross and had him run the names. I didn't tell him anything else."

"What are you hoping to find out?"

"Beats me," I said. "I'd be happy to get a decent clue that made sense."

Killian finished his eggs and wiped up the remaining yolk with a slice of toast. "None of this makes sense."

The phone rang. Ross's gravely voice sounded in my ear. "Your names belong to three guys who served in Special Forces."

"Really."

"Yes. One problem. They died five years ago. Long and Edwards in training accidents in Costa Rica, Adams in Panama. Only about a month apart."

"That's what I thought," I said. "Thanks, Jake."

"Anything I need to know, Logan?"

"Not that I'm aware of," I said and made a mental apology. I hung up and turned back to Killian.

"By the way, I haven't had time to tell you this until now. Teri cracked the code on the disk."

"And?"

"Hardaway. He's in this up to his ears. Teri says there's enough to put him away for life."

Killian seemed to take it all in. "Somehow that doesn't surprise me."

My cell rang. It was Karen. Her words sounded thick.

"John, get over here. They grabbed Tracy..."

"Who?"

"Just get over here."

26

I GOT TO KAREN'S PLACE TWENTY-TWO MINUTES LATER. Nothing seemed amiss, but Killian and I went quickly but cautiously to the door. We didn't wait to knock; we went in, guns at the ready.

"Where were you thirty minutes ago?"

Karen stood at the kitchen sink. There was a knot forming above her right eye and dried blood left a dark red track below her swollen bottom lip. A meal sat ready at the table, places set and even the wine glasses were filled.

"Jesus, Karen..." I went over to her. "What the hell happened?"

"Three men came in while we were getting ready to eat. They took Tracy. I tried to fight back—I took some bullshit self defense course a few years ago." She touched her lip. "Lot of good it did me."

"Did you get a look at them?"

"They wore masks and gloves but I did manage to bite one of them. Right on the hand. Once they had Tracy secured and me down, he took off his glove and wiped off the blood. There was a nightclub stamp on the back of his hand."

"A nightclub stamp?"

"Yeah, you know, they stamp you when you go in so you don't have to pay to get back in if you have to go outside. He had one."

"What club?"

"The Domino. I recognized the logo."

"They change those every night," Killian said, "with a different color so you can't use the one from the night before to get in free the next night."

"What color was it?"

"Purple. One more thing. He also had an accent. He said something when he was washing off the blood. Sounded like...boots."

"Boots?"

"That's what he said."

Silence erupted for a moment until Killian spoke the word slightly accented.

Karen snapped her fingers. "That's it."

Killian glanced at me. "Armenian."

"What does it mean?" Karen asked.

Killian stood motionless by the door. "It's not a nice term."

"You need to call the cops, Karen."

She ran a tongue across her swollen lip. "Gee, never thought of reporting a kidnapping, B and E, and an assault and battery." She glared. "I called your friend Jake Ross. He'll be here any minute."

I glanced at Killian. My friend seemed to read my mind.

"Do you need an ambulance?"

"I'm fine."

"Don't tell Ross you talked to me," I said, "if you can help it."

"What are you going to do?"

"I'm going back to my boat and let the cops handle it."

She looked at me then back to Killian. "Sure."

THE DOMINO CLUB was located on the Strip, a ten-block area of nightclubs, bars, and strip joints five blocks from the beachfront. It was a popular hangout for the wealthier kids who didn't have to work to afford their designer clothes and for middle-income kids who did have to work but had decided to blow their money on partying.

We were looking for an Armenian who'd been to the Domino Club recently. How recent would depend on the night they last used purple ink for their stamps.

Killian handled his Audi through traffic with expertise. We drove past sidewalks crammed with people dressed in Armani and others in blue jeans. Young women in mini-dresses and cleavage baring blouses hung onto guys with two hundred dollar haircuts and others with long hair and baggy pants. The streetlights glistened off metal piercings. The Strip, it was said, was a live lesson in human anthropology and behavior.

"You act like a man in familiar territory."

"You need to get out more often," Killian said.

"You know anyone at the Domino?"

My friend nodded. "I can find out."

"Low key, Kil. We can't let them know we're snooping."

"It's cool, bro." Killian parked the car in a small lot near the club. Behind the parking lot was a tattoo parlor housed in a two-story wooden frame home.

We made our way down the crowded sidewalk, squeezing past groups of teens and dodging through older kids who at first glared at us but turned away when Killian turned his dark sunglasses toward them.

The door attendant wore a tee shirt stretched tight over his body-builder frame and guarded the entrance to the Domino Club behind a velvet rope. A long line of hopefuls waited to try and get in. The doorman rolled his eyes as Killian and I went to the head of the line.

"Sorry. No can do." The guy raked Killian up and down. "The Armani jacket works, but it's just not hip enough tonight."

Killian held out a fifty. The man smiled. "Sorry. No can do."

"Pity," Killian said.

The doorman poked Killian in the chest. "I'm afraid you two need to try another night."

Killian's voice was low, down in the register he got when he was ready to get violent. "Touch me again and the money's off the table. Take it and let me and my friend pass."

"Look pal, I—" The door attendant's eyes widened. Killian gripped the man's wrist. I knew he'd be using the pressure point just inside the forearm near the wrist.

"Pity. You could have made fifty bucks." Killian stood as though there were nothing wrong in the world. He didn't move.

The doorman's mouth tried to work. His legs weakened; he began to sink, on his way to kneeling. Only when Killian let go did the fellow straighten up. He rubbed his wrist and I caught the glint of fear in his eyes.

"Thanks," Killian said and we walked through red double doors into a lobby that had only a sign for the restrooms. The carpet and wallpaper bore spots like—well, dominos.

"Cute," Killian said.

It was standing room only. The strobes and throbbing dance music reverberated off the walls. Killian and I split up. I spotted a familiar face leaning on a wall near the bathroom. He was a large fellow with a bald head and a serious stare. He wore a red Domino Club polo shirt.

"Hey Dave."

"John Logan, as I live and breathe." Dave Mulroney shook my hand.

"How's the police force?"

"Good. Working here for some extra cash." He continued to stare past me. "I'm watching that guy over there."

"You can rest easy, he's with me."

Dave's shoulders relaxed.

I said, "I need some info. When's the last time you guys used purple for your hand stamps?"

He thought. "Three nights ago."

"Remember any foreigners here that night?"

"Several were here. A couple of them are here tonight. I heard them talking earlier. Sounded like jibber jabber to me, maybe Russian."

"Where are they?"

Dave's eyes narrowed. "Is there going to be trouble, John?"

"Not if we can help it. Lady got roughed up tonight. A friend of mine I.D'd one of the people as Armenian. I want to talk to him."

"Just talk?"

I raised my hand. "Scout's honor."

"They were sitting in the far corner near the bar. Three of them."

"Thanks, Dave."

"No trouble, John. I'd hate to have to call the cops."

"Me, too. You can tag along if you like."

He smiled. "I think you and your friend can handle it."

"Thanks."

We spotted the table in a second. Three guys having a time. Two girls in short tight skirts with them. If we approached and confronted there'd be a scene, maybe a fight. Waiting until they left the club was preferable but I didn't know how long that would take. And time wasn't on my side. With Tracy kidnapped, every second might count. Karen had my cell number in case the kidnappers called, but I didn't think they would just yet.

I didn't know who they'd call, either. Tracy's family was dead so there was Karen or even me. It was a weak ploy for kidnapping. It didn't make sense to me unless you figured ransom wasn't their goal. There were other reasons to do a kidnapping. To extract information from the victim was one, or use the victim as bait to lure someone else to them was another.

"What do you think?" Killian said.

"Glasgow," I said.

"Thought you'd play it that way."

"Any better ideas?"

Killian thought. "Best way, I think. Besides, my Armenian's better."

"Way better."

We didn't have to wait long. One of the men got up and headed to the men's room. Killian slipped inside while I waited by the door. I stopped anyone entering by telling them that someone had thrown up all over the bathroom and they were cleaning it up. It would only be a few minutes but it smelled really bad in there. I got a few grumblings and a couple of drunken glares but otherwise there was no trouble.

Forty-five seconds after Killian went inside, I left my post and walked back out of the club. I went to the car and drove it around to an alley a block away. I sat, engine running, and waited. My Glock rested in my lap. I didn't know if these were low-level street hoods or experts. I didn't want to stake my life on either.

Killian showed with the Armenian in tow. He threw the guy into the backseat and climbed in beside him. The car moved before the back door fully closed. In the rearview mirror, I saw the man's frightened gaze meet mine, as though pleading with me to help him.

I can survive in Moscow if I have to but Killian was fluent in all the Slavic dialects. Killian spoke. The young man babbled something, his face the expression of pure sincerity and cooperation.

Killian punched him in the face.

The Russian jerked back against the door, blood coming from his nose.

"Everything okay?" I asked.

"Just bonding," Killian replied. "Logan, meet Vahan. A gallant name in his homeland. It means 'shield'.

I nodded into the rearview. "A pleasure."

Killian talked some more. Vahan shook his head. Killian shook his head. His left hand shot out and punched Vahan. The Armenian hit the door again. He couldn't fight back. Killian had zip tied his hands.

More talking.

I drove. My route took us across the bridge and to-ward the city. The lights made everything look pretty, harmless.

"Nice car," I said.

"Enjoy it while it lasts."

I knew what he meant. Killian would dispose of the car tonight in case Vahan's friends searched for him and managed to get a description.

There was a shout from the back. I glanced in the rearview. Killian held Vahan's leg and the muzzle of his Desert Eagle .44 Magnum rested against the side of the fellow's kneecap.

Although I didn't understand Armenian, I did know the tone of Killian's voice, that icy low tone that meant he was ready to do some nasty things.

The young man had more sense that I thought. He started talking, tears streaming down his face, mixing with the blood trickling from his nose and mouth. Killian listened. At last, the man shut up and slumped back against the seat. Killian eased the hammer down on the Magnum and slipped the cannon beneath his jacket.

"Vahan was the driver on the snatch. They handed her off to a group of Americans at an apartment house near 95," Killian said. "It may be just a holding area but that's where they last saw her. They could be gone by now."

"Yeah, but we have to check." I glanced in the mirrors and didn't see a tail. It didn't mean we didn't have one, only that I hadn't spotted it.

Vahan took us to an older neighborhood that existed before the city had grown to its current size. The noise of interstate traffic was audible.

The house was nothing special. Three stories, stucco exterior, stairs leading to the upstairs apartments. Maybe six units in all.

Vahan spoke.

"Second floor," Killian said. "On the right."

There was no moon and the street light was out by the house. Killian stuffed Vahan in the trunk. He didn't want to go but didn't argue. Killian has that effect on people.

That done, we glanced at each other. Time to check the apartment.

The thought that our friend might be leading us into a hornet's nest was not lost on me. Convince us that Tracy was here, we go barging in on an apartment full of angry Slavic fellows, and we end up dead. Slipping up the stairway, we paused at the door. Killian stuck his ear to the door, listened, and shook his head.

No sound from inside. The door was locked. Killian brought out his lock picking tools. It took him a couple of minutes.

"You're getting slow," I said.

"Something's not right."

"What?"

He shook his head and continued to work the tumblers.

"Talk to me, Kil."

"Don't know, bro. Just my gut."

It clicked into place and the handle turned. I went in first, Glock up and preparing for a fight.

The place was empty. A threadbare couch and overstuffed chair sat in the living room by a scarred coffee table. A small kitchen with only a few things in the pantry and nothing but a quart of milk in the fridge.

"Looks like a temporary stash house," Killian said.

My phone rang. It was Teri. "Where are you?"

I relayed current events. "We think they may have stashed her here temporarily."

"Wait," Teri said. "What's the address?"

I told her.

"Second floor, apartment on the right? Threadbare furniture?"

"Are you spying on us?"

"I forgot. You've been out of the business awhile. That's a Fed safe house."

"For whom?"

"Everyone. Bureau, NSA, even the Marshal Service uses it for Witness Protection."

Now it clicked. The windows and door were thicker. Bullet resistant. Killian had such a hard time with the locks because they weren't the normal residential locks.

"They've moved her again, Teri. We're trying to find her. Keep available. I may need you. Let me know if you hear anything. Any contact with the kidnappers?"

"None."

Killian was at the window, the Desert Eagle in his hand. "Bro, we're going to have company."

I looked out to see a squad of plainclothes men spill out of two black SUV's. They sported heavy-duty weaponry. I spotted large caliber pistols and H&K submachine guns. They checked the car. In a minute, they'd find our friend. I spotted one I recognized from the West Virginia woods. Buzz, from Cardigan Security; the one with the Sgt Rock jaw. He didn't look happy.

Killian stared out through the sunglasses. "Somehow I don't think they're Feds here to arrest us."

"They're not. They're part of the group that kidnapped me. Forsythe's security company."

Killian glanced around. He didn't need to say any-thing. We were sitting ducks here.

27

When I was a young Lieutenant, slogging my way through Green Beret training, an instructor at Fort Benning remarked that the gods of war have a sense of humor. They like to put you in a spot just to see if you have the chops to get out of it in one piece.

Killian and I were on a second floor apartment with no back door, and a squad of heavily armed men charging up the stairs. My friend held a small device in his hand.

"Is that what I think it is?"

"A diversion." He pressed the button and the earth shook as Killian's car exploded. Several bodies flew into the air; the rest fell down from the blast.

"Told you I would get rid of the car."

"Hope our friend was out of the trunk."

Killian didn't say anything. There was more shouting. He vanished down the hall while I checked the front door lock. Killian called out to me and I ran down the tiny hallway to the master bedroom. A sliding glass door on the far wall led to a small balcony on the rear facing side. A small barbecue grill sat in the corner of the balcony.

Killian kicked the lock and the door buckled. Another kick and it snapped. He slid the door aside and we went out.

The blast had surprised and confused the security men and no one was yet covering the back. We hung off the balcony and dropped. There was a six-foot privacy fence bordering the back yard and we scrambled for it. I was at the edge of the building when the first security man came around the corner, nearly colliding with me.

I reacted without thought. His weapon started up and I blocked the inside of his arm with my left. My right arm came out and caught him flush across the chest. He stopped as though hit by a wall; his legs flew from underneath him and he slammed on his back. Stunned, he shook his head. I hauled him to his feet and he stared at Killian's Magnum.

"Call Buzz back here," I said. "Don't make him suspicious. Anything else and my friend splatters your head like a melon."

Killian's aim was steady. "You sure you want to do this?"

"Yeah," I said, "he's mine. And he might know where they've taken Tracy."

The guy swallowed, slowly lifted his radio. "Buzz, come check this out."

Besides a slight tremor in his voice as he gazed at Killian's canon, his words were calm. Even. Not the slightest trace of excitement. If this guy ever decided to get out of the goon business, he'd make one hell of an actor.

Buzz ran into view. "What the hell do you—?"

He had just enough time to register my face before Killian brought the Magnum down across Buzz' head. He dropped like a rock. I knocked the other fellow out as well.

Killian didn't have to say anything. Buzz was my idea so I picked the fellow up in a fireman's carry and weaved through back yards. Killian called Teri and twenty minutes later, we deposited Buzz in the trunk of her car and drove away where Buzz and I could chat.

"EVER HEARD OF *KOPPO*, BUZZ?"

Buzz glared at me. Teri finished with the duct tape and Buzz was strapped tightly to the straight back chair. He wiggled and jerked, testing the bonds before glancing around at the vast emptiness. We were in an abandoned warehouse, one of many near the docks along the bay.

"Yeah, I know. Empty and deserted. No one for blocks," I said.

"What the hell do you want? I'm not afraid of you."

"Where's Tracy Rochelle?"

He smiled. "Go screw yourself, Logan."

I held up a finger. "*Koppo* is actually a sub discipline of ninjutsu. I'm talking the actual ninja arts, Buzz, not the Hollywood crap you see. Anyway, *Koppo* refers to the art of breaking bones. Breaking them, dislocating them, oh, it hurts like hell." I walked over and grabbed the fingers of his right hand. "Where's Tracy Rochelle?"

He breathed heavy, as though he'd run hard. Fear made you do that, the body's response to stress. Sweat gathered along his hairline.

"There are two hundred and six bones in the human body, not counting the tiny ones in the ear and such," I said. "I can break every one of them. When I'm done, I'm turning you over to her—" I gestured at Teri. "Her favorite thing is to take a model knife and cut you in—well personal areas."

"You're psycho, Logan."

"Tracy Rochelle, Buzz. Next time I have to ask you, I break a finger."

"They'll kill me..."

"You told me in West Virginia you were going to kill me." I leaned in close to his face. "Now tell me why I shouldn't slowly take you apart. Your only way of walking out of here is to tell me where she is."

His head dropped. He was screwed and he knew it. He could be brave and let me work on him awhile, but in the end, he'd tell me and he knew it. "She's at the beach house. Where Forsythe bought it."

"Hardaway?"

He nodded. "He thinks she might know something about where her old man stashed the file."

"What file?"

"The file that her dad was building on the whole operation. If it got out, Hardaway and the guys above him would fry."

"Above him? Hardaway isn't in charge?"

"No. There's someone else."

"Who?"

"I don't know. Never met him or them. I don't know."

"How'd you know about the apartment?"

"We got told to go there. Said there was a breach in the place and it was probably you."

"Who told you? Hardaway?"

Buzz nodded. "He had us go to the old man's house in Baltimore. Rummage through it with a fine toothcomb. Hell, we didn't even know if we'd know it if we found it. We got nothing. The girl is Hardaway's panic move. He's afraid someone will find that file."

I walked away. "Consider yourself lucky that I'm just leaving you here tied up. It's a better option than you were going to leave me."

"It was never personal, Logan. I read your file. I also heard you let my man go. I appreciate that."

"I see you again on opposite sides, Buzz, and all bets are off."

We left him tied up in the warehouse.

"MAYBE WE SHOULD HAVE KILLED HIM," Teri said.

We lay on a sand dune just down the beach, Teri and I looking through night vision binoculars at the house where James Forsythe had met his demise. I'd wondered why they'd chosen to bring Tracy here but the beach house made sense. The safe house was in an apartment building. It's hard to hide that many guns or stifle the sounds of torturing someone when there's an apartment next door. The same with a hotel room. The house had a natural defense on the east side. Anyone coming in would have to ingress through the water or along the beach. Easy to spot.

"I made a decision." I hoped that sparing Buzz wouldn't come back to bite me later.

She scanned the beach. "You think he's going to try you sometime?"

"We'll see."

The ocean roared in our ears. Wispy clouds covered the moon, making it shimmer in the sky. Elsewhere, people were watching the late news, sleeping, or making love.

"I count two SUV's," I said.

Killian sounded in my left ear. "Three roving guards on the perimeter, one on the deck. They look bored."

Killian was perched in a tree to our left and slightly behind us. He had a view of the deck and the windows on the south side. It wasn't the ideal spot for sniping but it was the best that we had on short notice.

Satisfied the beach was clear, Teri turned her attention back to the house. "Where'd you get that rifle, Mason? It's awesome."

"Cracker Jacks," Killian responded. "There's a prize in every box."

Teri frowned. "Tell me again why I'm not on the rifle providing overwatch?"

"Because I need you to take care of Tracy and get her out of there," I said. "I don't know what kind of condition she'll be in and your field medicine was always top notch."

Teri grunted. "Did you just give me a compliment?"

"I'll check the officer's manual later."

"There's a car pulling up," Teri said.

We raised our binoculars. Another SUV pulled up to the house. Franklin Hardaway got out of the car and went inside.

Killian whispered, "The rat bastard himself."

I kept scanning the house. It didn't change the plan. "Only one way in through the ground level, a door underneath the deck near the driveway. Then a tight corkscrew stairway up to the living room."

"Not the best place for an entry."

It was an understatement. The stairway allowed for only single file access. It didn't permit fast or quiet ascension.

"Only one other way."

Teri sighed. "I was afraid you would say that."

We did a quick check. We were in black; my Glock rested on my hip. I had a knife sheathed to my chest and a telescoping baton taped to my left forearm. Teri had a Beretta 9mm holstered in the small of her back as well as a baton.

She had a field medical kit tucked into the cargo pocket of her pants.

"Are we clear?"

There was a heartbeat before Killian answered. "Go."

"Moving."

We ran toward the house. The deck extended out over the frame by five feet, supported with wooden pillars sank into the sand. It was only a hundred yards but it seemed like a mile. We made it underneath the deck, backs against the frame of the house.

Teri winked. "Just like Somalia."

Killian whispered in my ear. "One guard at the rail, looking east."

I climbed up one of the support ties and reached out, grabbed the floor of the deck and prayed I wouldn't slip. Using my upper body to pull up to where I could reach a railing, I grabbed the bottom rail and pulled myself up. I was going over the railing when the guard turned and spotted me. It took him a second to register that there was a man climbing onto the deck. There wasn't time for him to see anything more. He jerked and went down. I never heard a shot from Killian's suppressed rifle.

"Very nice," Teri whispered. She climbed up and over the rail and we were in.

We started toward the sliding glass doors. We didn't have to bother. The door slid open and Franklin Hardaway appeared with three Cardigan Security men surrounding him, guns drawn on us.

"Logan," He grinned, "what kept you?"

28

From the onset, it had been a risky operation. To think that we could sneak in to a beach house filled with armed men and rescue Tracy was crazy. They frisked and disarmed us before leading us inside. Hardaway was grinning like a cat. I spotted Barlow in the corner and Buzz at the bar. Neither one looked at me.

"Does your partner know you're here?" I asked Barlow.

"She's too straight of an arrow," the Fed replied. "Someone had to watch her."

"Are you in this for the thrill or love of country?"

Barlow rubbed thumb and forefinger together. "The money. You could have been smart and played ball but you decided to try and be the hero."

"So, you sold your badge."

"Wasn't much to sell. The Bureau's a mess these days."

There was the clink of ice as Hardaway refreshed his drink. "I suppose you're here for Bill's little girl, huh? Let me show her to you." With guards keeping a close eye on me, I followed Hardaway to one of the bedrooms. Tracy lay on the bed, her body racked with spasms.

"What did you do to her?"

"Oh we pumped her full of heroin and got her addiction back in full swing. Now she wants more and she's not getting it until she tells us where the file is."

"She doesn't know. Bill never told her."

Hardaway frowned. "And you know this how?"

"Because I have it."

Hardaway's eyes widened and then he chuckled. "A weak bluff, Logan."

"I don't think so." My stomach sank as David Chang walked into the living room. I heard Teri gasp in surprise.

"Where'd you find it, John?"

"What are you doing here, David?"

"Surprised? Bill had everything on Franklin here but he was still searching for the upper man, the one he suspected was pulling the good Senator's strings. I couldn't let him find out."

It became clear to me. "It was you. You killed Bill."

He nodded. "I lay in the back of his yard and called him. Coerced him to look out at his pool. You know what they say about curiosity and the cat, right?"

I forced the words out. "You walked him right to his death."

"A brilliant masterpiece, don't you think?"

"Forsythe, too?"

He smiled. "Snuck in the house and waited. Hell, Frankie there showed up and didn't even suspect I was around. I stood in that closet and watched Bill's daughter screw like a porn star. Everyone left and she went to the can...then it was easy. I stepped out and ran the sword through him. He died quietly, but struggling." David's face darkened. "He betrayed me. I wanted to send a message out for anyone who might have wanted to betray me. I also sent it as a warning to Bill to drop this. I didn't want to have to kill him but he wouldn't stop." David's face grew dark. "Where did you find the file?"

"In Bill's desk hidden in the back of a picture."

David shook his head. "Rent-a-cops couldn't find their ass with both hands."

"You're using the unit to smuggle drugs."

"Drugs, weapons, hell the U.S. is the largest arms dealer in the world," David said. "I'm just helping things out and getting rich in the meantime right under Congress' nose. Serves them right for slashing budgets and turning the unit into a CIA puppet. Exactly what Bill didn't want to ever happen."

"You were the Grinkov leak. You were the one who told them we were coming. Where we would be. That's how they knew."

"He had some interests in the world. I took them over." He smiled. David Chang's smile was the cold kind, like the smile of a salesman right before he screws you on your new car.

"What about the team? Gina and the rest?"

"If the truth got out, I knew you guys would come for me. I decided to be proactive and get you all out of the way. That way Bill couldn't use you to help him."

"We trusted you," Teri said.

"Never trust anyone in this business." David looked at us. "Oh, I'm sorry. Are you two an item again? That was the worst kept secret in the office, John."

Teri's eyes flashed defiance. David walked over to her. "I'm going to enjoy you later, Teri."

"I've gotten better offers from fat drunken Russians."

He grabbed her chin with his hand. She started to resist

but the guns came up close. "Just for that, I'm going to show you the connection between pain and pleasure."

She returned his stare.

I had to try to focus him back onto me. "Why did Bill go to Forsythe?"

David stared into Teri's eyes for a moment before loosening his grip. He turned away with a lecherous gleam in his eye. "Bill knew he needed additional help in getting to the truth. He couldn't trust Langley with their incompetence and leaks. He also knew I'd find out. He went to the only other person he knew who had the resources. Forsythe was a patriot and an old friend. Except Forsythe was up to his ears and Bill never knew it. Forsythe was going to spill the beans to Bill. He wasn't a completely willing participant in this scheme."

"What's your part in all of this, Franklin?"

"I made sure his buyouts of foreign companies got pushed cleanly through Congress," Hardaway said. "This one for MicroCorp—well it was a biggie. Forsythe needed it. His last couple of deals hadn't panned out very well. MicroCorp promised to be a big boom for him."

"And what did you do?"

"I asked him to make a special run for me," Hardaway said. "A nice haul this time. A quarter ton of high-grade Golden Crescent horse." The Senator shrugged slightly. "Of course, there was always the problem of coming back into U.S. waters, customs and all of that. But we paid off the right people to get it done."

"Forsythe was going to squeal so you killed him. And you killed Bill because he knew about it all." I turned to David. "How'd he manage to find it all out?"

"He was a bloodhound, you know that."

"You tried to kill off the team, David. Even me. Too bad

the person you sent didn't do the job. I'm surprised you saved me for last."

Hardaway laughed. David Chang stared at me.

"He doesn't know," Hardaway said.

"I tried for you first, John. Remember Paris?"

Everything seemed to freeze. "That was a terrorist cell operation. You gave me the info on them—" I felt sick as the realization dawned on me. I had fallen victim to one of the best tricks in the spy trade. I'd let David supply me with intelligence on those responsible for the Paris blast and I'd killed them. My knees weakened until it was a Herculean effort to keep upright. My stomach rolled. I started toward him but guns pointed at me. A muzzle pushed into my cheek, forcing me back. I had to work to slow my rapid breathing.

"I think he's got a grasp of it now." Hardaway said.

"I'm going to kill you..."

"She was in the wrong place at the wrong time," Chang said. "You had to ruin it. Had to get up and walk across the damn street. Karma, eh?"

"Bet you were surprised to learn I'd survived."

"I was," David replied. "But then again, you always had a knack for beating the odds."

My hands clenched. "I'm going to kill you, David."

"No, you're not." He crossed his arms in front of his chest. "I have to admit, seeing you run all over the globe, taking out bad guys, watching Langley try to rein you in. Damn better than a movie, but it's finished, John. You gave it a hell of a run, but in the end, you should have walked away and let this go."

Hardaway stood near the bar. I took a deep breath and looked over at him. My legs felt weak and I was close to the point of throwing up, sick at how I'd let myself be used.

I forced the feelings away. I had to focus on the situation at hand. "So this is how you want to be remembered, Franklin? Someone who betrayed his office because of dope?"

"My office?" Hardaway asked. "Let me tell you about my office, Logan. About being a Senator in this great republic. Do you know what we do all day? Do you know what our great government does all day? Everything is geared to doing to the one thing the American people want us to do."

"And what is that?"

"To provide them with more shit to buy. Americans want cheap gas for their big cars, they want cheap TV's and DVD players, and they want unlimited credit. They don't care if the books balance or if soldiers are sent to the Middle East. Oh, sure, they wave the flag and put the support the troops stickers on their cars and they talk about what a great job the soldiers do in protecting their freedoms. Freedoms, my ass. We all know the soldiers are over there so we can have gas in our tanks. We meet with dictators and psychopaths and shake hands and smile and let the cameras flash so their countries will continue to pay their workers slave wages so we can have cheap toys for our kids and digital this and that. All coming to your local stores at a high price, Logan. A very high price." He took a long swallow of his drink. "When I was a kid, America was the world's producer, baby. The world bought from us. Now we buy from them. Because they produce it cheap and that's what America wants. We had to sell everyone on the importance of international trade and a world economy so they'd feel better about buying clothes made in a factory in Bangladesh by a ten-year-old kid working sixteen hours a day for two dollars."

"You're in a position to change it. Your run for the Oval Office, remember?"

He laughed. "Change it? How? Americans don't want to change it, Logan. Remember Carter? He came on TV, said that our growing dependence on foreign oil was a threat to national security, and encouraged conservation and investment in alternative energies. He was derided and laughed out of office. He ran against Reagan who called Carter a negative naysayer, that it was morning in America, and our best days were ahead. And stupid Americans bought it." He waved it aside. "I'm gonna give them more of the same. Do a term and retire. Get my pension and make a nice living from my other—" He looked around. "Investments."

"You mean drug money."

"Money is money, boy," Hardaway said, "no matter how you get it."

"You won't get elected being involved in this stuff."

"Oh I will. I can guarantee it. Your protégé Chang—well, he's a real D.C. whiz kid. He's better than Hoover digging up stuff on people. By the time he's done anyone who thinks about opposing my nomination will swiftly change their minds. And once I'm in, I'm gonna take Bill Rochelle's old unit and make it formidable again. David will have carte blanc to run all over the world and kill any sonofabitch who even thinks about blowing up an American. I help him. He helps me. It's a win-win for all of us."

"In the meantime, you're not only going to be a party to drug smuggling but murder as well."

Hardaway spread his arms. "I tried to warn you, Major."

David sighed. "Where's the file. John?"

"No idea."

"You're lying." Chang came in close. "You give me the file and Bill's little girl gets rid of the shakes."

I sighed and lowered my head, the very picture of a man defeated. "I'm afraid I did something stupid with it."

"What's that?" Hardaway asked.

"I turned it over to the local police and FBI."

Hardaway's face fell. "You did..."

"Yeah," Teri said. "He did."

David shook his head. "That was a damn fool thing to do."

"Sorry."

David walked away. "Keep Miss Johnson alive. Buzz, shoot Logan."

Buzz looked him in the eye. "No, sir."

David stopped. "What?"

"He could have killed me in the warehouse but he didn't. He also could have killed us in the woods that time. I owe him one. Soldier to soldier."

"I can understand that—" David's hand moved with a cobra's speed, under his jacket. A pistol came out and he fired. Buzz jerked and dropped to the floor. He struggled for a moment to bring his weapon up, but the light faded from his eyes and he let out a final breath and was still.

Then a window blew out. The unfortunate man standing in front of it seemed to explode and fly across the room. Before anyone could react, another window broke and a man went down.

"Sniper!" Someone yelled and all hell broke loose.

29

Everything happened in a blur. Barlow went into a crouch and pulled his weapon. I grabbed the nearest soldier and put him between Barlow and me. Simultaneously grabbing the soldier's gun hand, I wrenched his Taurus .40 caliber free and felt him shudder as Barlow's shots tore into him. I shoved the dying man away and went into a moving crouch, pistol firing.

Hardaway suddenly gasped, clutching his stomach. Another shot rang out from somewhere to my left and Hardaway dropped. I was still moving as guns were pulled. I shot Barlow twice in the chest, took his pistol, and capped one thug pulling hardware from beneath a suit jacket. Teri had disappeared into the melee.

More shots outside now. I dove behind a sofa as pieces of stuffing and fabric flew skyward. A bullet ripped completely through and exited out, barely missing my stomach. I used the space between couch and floor, firing underneath and hitting feet and ankles until the damn slide locked back and I sprinted like mad for a love seat on the far wall. More men lay on the floor, some dead, others with bad wounds. Some had already tried to escape.

Grabbing another pistol off the floor, I looked around for more bad guys. And there were plenty still around. Chang had an army. One goon stood at the top of the stairs shooting at me. Jesus, couldn't he see that I had just finished a fight and I needed a breather? I scooted toward the love seat firing two shots at my attacker. A bullet tore through the love seat and exited in a shower of fabric and I felt something hot graze my leg. I grabbed a fallen Glock, slid too far, and my head popped out from the other end. There was a loud boom and I expected to get a bullet in the head; I fired and started to roll away but the shooter was already falling face first. Teri stood behind him. She held a pistol in a combat stance.

"You okay?"

"Yeah." I started to my feet. "Get Tracy."

She started to the back. More movement to the right. "Teri!" I shouted but there was no need. Both shooters went down from someone else.

Killian came in from the deck. My friend wielded two Desert Eagle .44 Magnum semi-automatics, the big ones with ventilated barrels. He wore his sunglasses and moved across the room with the grace of a panther.

"You okay?"

"I'm grazed but I'm fine," I said. "You're a tad late."

"Took a dip in the ocean." Killian said. Another Cardigan thug had found his way through the other door and stumbled into the room. He spotted us and started to bring his pistol up.

Killian's left arm came out in a firing range stance, as calm as though he were shooting at paper targets instead of a live human being trying to kill him. The Magnum boomed a hell of a roar; the 250-grain slug picked the hapless fellow off his feet and deposited him in a bloody heap in the corner. Another came behind him. I doubled-tapped shots into him and he bounced out of sight.

"Nicely done, old chap," Killian said in a mock British accent.

Ross suddenly appeared, pistol drawn, followed by a group of Federal agents led by Kim Healy. The agents fanned out and began to clear the house.

"You certainly brought enough back-up."

Killian's face was expressionless. "It's a joint jurisdictional cooperative thing or something like that."

Healey gave only a glance at Barlow.

"I'm sorry," I said.

"Doesn't matter to me," she said and went through the opposite door.

Ross looked around. Amidst the bodies, blood splattered the carpet and walls. The far wall bore two large holes from Killian's rifle. There was an occasional gunshot.

"Jesus," he said.

Killian holstered the Magnums in the double shoulder rig he wore. "No. Remington and Colt."

"There's another problem," Ross said. "David Chang got away."

"You'll see him again," Killian said to me.

I nodded and looked around at the carnage.

"I DON'T LIKE THIS." Teri glared at me.

"I know," I said. "But we have no choice."

"I get that," she said. "But let me help you."

"There's no one I'd rather have in a fight than you," I said. "But this is between me and him."

"Why is it so personal, John?"

"He killed Shikira."

"And also Gina, Mallory, and the others. They were my friends, too."

"It's my duty to fix this, Teri."

"But why?"

"I recruited him. Trained him."

For a moment, she said nothing. Then, "I didn't know that."

"Not something I'm proud of given how he turned out."

She paused. "You know, there was another reason I came here...to Coral Bay."

"What?"

"I came here to watch you."

"Watch me?"

"Langley contacted me. They thought you might be behind the killings of the team. With your rampage after Shikira's death, they had their suspicions about you. They thought you might be behind the others' deaths. I didn't believe them. Then those creeps came after me. I didn't know what to think. I called Langley and they told me to come here and see if I could get evidence against you."

"You thought I'd killed the others? You thought I sent those men after you?"

Teri got up and marched toward the door. She stopped before walking out. She turned to me, her eyes wet and her jaw clenched in the way she did when she was mad. "I'm sorry. I should have trusted you." The door slammed and she was gone.

東

Two days passed. I slept and worked on the boat. On the second night, it seemed normal...the boat rocking on the water, the distant noise of cars and an occasional siren. The muted sounds of laughter and music from a bay front restaurant came across the water. People out with friends and family, laughing and celebrating life while I prepared to die.

Maybe.

He didn't even rock the boat when he clambered on board and I hadn't bothered locking the door in those two days. I wanted him to find it unlocked, to know that I expected him to be there, wanted him to question how surprised I really would be that he was there.

I came out of the head toward the galley.

"I knew you would make it out of the house." He waited for me, sitting in the dark like a Buddha.

"Is that why you left?"

David shrugged. "You did me another favor. Hardaway was becoming a liability. All this talk about running for office. Once again, John, you cleaned up my mess."

"And the others?"

"Expendable assets."

"Hardaway wanted to restore the unit to its former glory."

"I don't want it anymore," David replied. "I'm getting rich."

Anger welled inside me and for a moment, the only sound was my pulse pounding in my ears. Something flashed in my vision just before he barreled into me, sending me sprawling onto the floor. My shoulder banged against the edge of the bar. I tried to roll out but he was ready for me and hammered his fist down toward my cheek. I brought up my arms, taking the punch on the forearm, feeling the blow all the way to my shoulder. Got my right arm up between the side of his face and shoulder and elbowed him in the cheek once, twice, three times, before twisting right and getting him off me. We were on our feet; David attacked with a savage combination of kung fu and *savate*, French foot fighting. I blocked the shots, the assault driving me backwards; each blow smashing into my arms that I knew would be bruised tomorrow. I stepped into him and hammered three punches to his face, staggering him. He countered with two of his own before spinning in a vicious back kick that caught me in the chest, sending me tumbling over the sofa. I rolled to my feet, arms up in a defensive posture, but a blow got through. A kick caught me under the chin, snapping my jaw shut. Light exploded in my vision and the floor rose up to smack me. The coppery taste of blood filled my mouth. I was on my hands and knees trying to get up when David suddenly lunged on me. His weight pressed me to the floor, arms trying to snake around my neck.

"Time to die, John," he said. "The days of glory are over for you. They're dead, just like your Jap wife."

There will be a time, Funichi once told me, *when death stares you in the face. When your mortality comes at you and there is no time to think, no time to ponder. Only to find the strength to push it away and fight on.*

I screamed, a *kiai* shout that reverberated through the room. Blackness formed at the edges of my vision, threatening to seep further in until there was nothing. The calmness of the warrior was gone, replaced only by an inhuman rage that tore through my being. My arms were free and I brought them back, driving my elbows into his floating ribs repeatedly, hearing his grunts of pain in my ear, ignoring the pain of my battered body. His grip loosened for a second and I dug my thumb and forefinger into the nerve junction just inside the elbow, my other hand clawing for the pressure point at his wrist. I felt him loosen further and I twisted, shoving him off me. He rolled aside and I went atop him, smashing an elbow into his face. I worked by feel and instinct, the primeval taking over in the ages old battle to survive. There was a crack as his nose splintered and something warm and wet splattered my face but I no longer cared. There was only the enemy before me.

I got to my feet, blood pounding in my ears. I kicked him in the ribs with savage fury, feeling the bones break beneath his skin.

"How much did they pay you to set us up, David?"

"No one paid me," he said. Blood poured from his nose and he made no effort to wipe it away. He staggered to his feet. "I saw an opportunity...an investment. And why not? What difference did it make in the end, John? We toppled one dictator and another would sprout up. We caught one terrorist and three more strap C4 to their chest. In the end, it made no difference. Grinkov was selling weapons, yeah, but so were half a dozen people a lot bigger than he was. You just cut off one finger from a very big body."

Hadn't I told Bill the same thing? "Your teammates died, David. People who trusted you."

He looked around. "You could have some of it, John. Move up a little in the world. With Hardaway gone, it's just me now. You could be a rich man."

"I'm not for sale," I said. "You killed my wife, David."

"You can get a thousand more like her."

My answer was a guttural growl containing months of pain and hurt. "There'll never be another like her."

"Such a damned sentimentalist." He darted left, and I followed him. He passed the teakwood table and snatched the katana, pulling blade and sheath apart in one fluid motion. He came at me quickly, blade flashing out. I ripped off my shirt and waited until he was committed to a slice and threw the shirt in his face.

It only distracted him for a second but it was all I needed. I got inside his defenses, four hands struggling for the blade and it scooted aside. We stood trading blows, arms and legs moving in combinations and pat-terns created centuries before. I grabbed his arm, flipped him in mid air. He crashed down and rolled toward the katana. I grabbed the smaller blade—the *wakizashi*—from the table; one, two, three strides toward him, pulling the shorter sword free, bringing it down horizontally to block his attack and guide the blade downward and right, spinning right, outside the katana's path, bringing the shorter blade in a horizontal path into his side.

He screamed and staggered. I withdrew the blade and he stood unsteadily, looking at me with those black eyes. Blood oozed from his mouth and he managed a faint smile.

I ran the blade into him, just below the sternum. He gasped and made a choking sound.

"That's for Bill," I said.

Blood oozed from his mouth. David grinned. His mouth worked but the words didn't come. I pulled upward on the blade, feeling it slice into flesh and bone.

"That's for the team."

I pulled the blade free and he dropped to the floor. Lucky mewed from beneath the sofa. I grabbed the katana. David watched through dying eyes, already knowing.

"This is for Shikira—" I brought the sword out in a flash of steel and David's headless corpse sank to the floor.

Sirens sounded in the distance. I could do nothing but crumple to the floor in tears, battered and exhausted.

30

A PUBLIC MEMORIAL SERVICE FOR JAMES FORSYTHE WAS HELD at the St. Paul's Catholic Church near the bay front. Coral Bay's golden boy was buried in a private ceremony much earlier, but the city leaders thought it best that the city and the public be able to pay their respects to a man who had done a lot for his community.

Emily Forsythe sat in the front pew, flanked by her two children. It was the first time I had seen them. They resembled their mother but the son had his father's eyes.

City and state leaders filled the place. The Governor and mayor were there and both spoke of Forsythe as an inspiration and pillar to his community. The Vice President of the Forsythe Group also eulogized Coral Bay's favorite son, mentioning Forsythe's integrity and commitment to his country. Emily Forsythe looked over at me. Our eyes met and she mouthed *thank you.*

Teri sat beside me. "I guess Forsythe's extracurricular activities are not being disclosed to the public?"

"No. Dana Costello wasn't happy about it but we

convinced her and her bosses that it would compromise national security if the truth came out."

"Doesn't seem right in a way."

"He wasn't a completely willing participant. I think it's better this way."

"He did a lot of good for the city."

"We do the best we can and hope that it is enough."

Teri slipped an arm under mine. "Are you saying that for his benefit or for yours?"

I didn't answer.

"You're a good man, John Logan."

"Thanks, T."

"What about me?"

I looked over at her. "What about you?"

"Do you forgive me?"

"What you did, you did for the team. There is nothing to forgive. I would have done the same."

I glanced around. Ross and members of the police department stood near the back. The cop caught my eye and gave me a slight nod.

Teri asked, "What about your FBI girl?"

"She's not my girl. She was given a commendation for her work. Barlow was buried with his name, I guess. I didn't check."

She nodded. Hardaway's death sent rumblings through Washington and Langley was still chafing about my involvement. When I threatened to expose the fact that they had ignored Bill's warnings about David, they'd backed off. But they still weren't happy with me.

"I wonder sometimes."

"About what?" Teri asked.

"If I'm really a good man."

"You are. You were a good leader."

"I wasn't a good husband. I was gone too much."

"Shikira was proud of you," Teri said. "Remember the time you had a bunch of us over for a cookout?"

"Wow, I forgot about that."

"I talked to Shikira then," Teri said. "It was the only time I ever did. She talked about you and your life together. She said she wouldn't trade it for any other."

For a moment in time, the separation vanished. I felt Shikira beside me. It made me shiver and sent a chill up my spine. Then it was gone.

"Everyone I've ever loved has left me," I said.

"I won't leave you."

"I still love her, Teri."

"I know."

"And you still want to be around me?"

"We'll take it a day at a time and see what happens. If you can forgive me."

I couldn't ask for anything else. "There's nothing to forgive."

東

"MY BOSS CAN'T BELIEVE this story," Ross said "To think that Forsythe was involved in smuggling." The cop wore a cheap blue suit, contrasting sharply with Killian's black Versace suit and red tie. Ross took a swallow of his beer. "The Bureau is still assessing the damage from Barlow's actions. The DEA's getting involved in the arrangements in Aruba as well. How're Karen and Tracy?"

We were at an upscale Italian place near the bay front. Teri looked splendid in a violet cocktail dress.

I helped myself to a dish of fried calamari. "Karen's back to work and Tracy...well, I haven't seen her."

"Hard to believe that David was behind it all those years," Teri said. "Imagine what Bill must have felt when he found out."

"Imagine his surprise," I said. "And his anger. David had pulled one over on him. And that wouldn't set too well with Bill. He finds out that his agents are dying and tells Gina. Gina, knowing she has no one to talk about it with and knowing that she might be next, calls up her old friend, Healey. Tells her what she can over the phone. Now, David finds out the FBI is snooping. He gets his man Barlow assigned as her partner."

"Well, my captain is patting me on the back so hard he might hurt his hand." Ross took a bite of the calamari. "I've got a lot of paperwork to do." He looked at me. "I owe you another one, Logan."

"You owe me nothing, Jake."

"If you hadn't meddled, that girl would have been locked up for life."

"I owed it to her father."

"And so Chang killed Forsythe?"

I nodded. "Sneaked into the house and waited. Even Hardaway didn't know he was there. When he saw Tracy go to the restroom, he slipped out and drove the sword home. Nice and professional."

"Bill found out your Asian friend is dirty and he ends up going to Forsythe for help."

I nodded. "Forsythe and Bill go back years. Bill knew he'd need help tracking David's activities down and Forsythe had the connections and the resources. What Bill didn't know was that Forsythe was involved in David's criminal organization. When he told Forsythe what he discovered, he sealed his fate. David would surely find out. When

David finds out, he starts killing members of Bill's old unit as a warning to Bill to back off."

"Except Bill didn't do it." Teri said.

"David also suspected, I think, that Forsythe was going to spill his guts to Bill. Forsythe was loyal to his close friends, in spite of his flaws. He couldn't betray Bill and David knew it. So Forsythe invites Hardaway down to his yacht to discuss the MicroCorp deal and David sees his chance. He finds out Bill's girl is Forsythe's mistress and that she has a drug problem. Tracy becomes his scapegoat. David kills Forsythe, then Bill."

"I thought killing Forsythe with the sword might have been an attempt to frame you," Killian spoke up.

"Perhaps," I nodded. "At least give the police another rabbit to chase. Fortunately, they had a good man on the job."

"Whatever," Ross said. "I'm just an underpaid civil servant."

Teri sipped her wine. "What about Emily Forsythe?"

Ross chuckled. "She's taking over her husband's company from what I hear and cooperating fully with the authorities in digging through all of her husband's dealings. The Forsythe Group will be a lot smaller by the time the books are balanced."

"What about MicroCorp?" Killian asked.

I took another bite. "That deal is probably dead in the water."

"Chang was using products from the same company that Forsythe was trying to buy," Killian shook his head. "Did Forsythe know?"

"Probably not. He was already dead before we started getting bugged. But Forsythe would have done his homework on the company. David had to get the equipment from somewhere and he had all the knowledge of their products through Forsythe's research."

"Doesn't seem right though, all of this being kept under wraps from the public," Teri said. "How'd they treat Hardaway?"

Ross answered, "Officially, heart attack."

I sipped my beer. "The system can work wonders when it needs to."

"Speaking of which," Ross said to Teri. "The police in California are not going to be seeking to press charges on you for the two bodies on the beach, given the facts. You're free to go back home, Ms Johnson."

"Thanks, Lieutenant, but I might stay. I kinda like it here." Teri said, looking at me. "Besides, you can use a partner."

"I already have one." I gestured at Killian.

"You can use me. Admit it, I come in handy."

"You do."

"And she's cuter than you," Killian said.

THREE DAYS after the memorial service, I looked up from the morning paper to find Emily Forsythe standing on the dock. She wore khaki shorts and a white sleeveless blouse.

"This is a surprise."

"So, this is where a private investigator lives."

"Not all of them," I said. "Just me."

She stepped on board. I expected Lucky to hiss at her but he stayed curled up on an old pillow.

"I hope I'm not catching you at a bad time."

"Not at all, I'm just enjoying the sunshine."

She looked out across the water. "It is beautiful this morning, isn't it?"

"Yes, it is." The water was a deep blue. A flock of birds flew overhead in a V formation and the city smelled clean and new, as though it had been reborn from the ashes of the past events. "How are you doing?"

"I'm fine," she said. "I miss him more than I thought I would."

"I understand that."

"I heard that your wife was killed last year."

"Yes."

"I'm sorry." Emily glanced at me when she said it then turned her eyes back onto the water. "Does it ever go away?"

"What?"

"Loving them."

"If it does, I'll let you know." I gestured toward the chairs. "What brings you out my way?"

She accepted my offer of a seat. "I just wanted to say thank you for everything. Jim was buried, his name untarnished. I appreciate that."

"What about your kids?"

"They don't know, of course. Probably best that they remember their dad in a positive light. They didn't have many positive things to remember him by anyway."

"If it makes you feel any better, Mrs. Forsythe—"

"Emily."

"Emily, your husband was not a completely willing participant in this ordeal. He was killed because he was going to tell Bill Rochelle everything."

"Is that why you decided to keep this under wraps?"

"We all do stupid things, Emily. Your husband was far from perfect but he tried to help Bill. Since I owe my old friend so much, I figured helping your husband is enough for me."

"Thank you."

"What about you?"

"The Forsythe Group is on shaky ground financially. The deal with MicroCorp is still a possibility and I'm hopeful it will go through."

"The board approved you?"

"Yes."

"I'm glad things are working out for you," I said. "If you ever need an investigator—"

She smiled. "I'll give you a call." She stood and reached out a hand. "Thank you again, Mr. Logan."

I took her hand in a firm handshake; she leaned over and gave me a quick kiss on the mouth.

"That's so I don't wake up in the night wondering," she said. She stepped off the boat and headed down the pier. The last glance I got of her was an impossibly long leg getting into a car.

For a moment, I sat looking at the water.

I did it. I got the ones responsible. I hope you can rest now, baby. I miss you.

東

TWO WEEKS LATER, I climbed out of my car to see Ross standing at the entrance to an apartment house. The neighborhood was decaying, the buildings old and tired. There were already plenty of emergency vehicles here and I knew I wasn't going to like what was inside. I didn't realize how much that dislike would be.

"What's up, Jake?"

"Thought you'd want to see this." The detective's face was a mask of anger kept under sheer control. "Come on."

"What is it?"

He didn't answer me. We walked into the foyer and up a flight of stairs that creaked. I was expecting them to give in at any minute.

"Got a call from the landlord," he said. We hit the top landing and hung a right. There was an open door. Crime scene technicians worked inside.

The apartment was tiny and sparsely furnished. I saw a battered and threadbare sofa, a straight back chair and a beanbag covered in several makeshift patches of duct tape. The place smelled of reefer, sweat, and cheap beer.

A dead person sprawled on the sofa, one leg on the floor, the other draped on the arm. He couldn't have been more than nineteen. There was white froth bubbling around his mouth, his eyes half-open, staring sightlessly at his last moment of life.

We went by the bedroom and I saw the body of a female. She lay on her side as though she were sleeping. A technician snapped photos for the crime scene file.

"In here," Ross said and opened the bathroom door.

She lay in the bathtub, in shorts and tee. Her head lolled to one side and her eyes were closed. One hand hung over the tub and a hypodermic needle lay an inch from her fingertips. Her nails were painted a deep red.

Oh, Jesus...

"Looks like they got a bad batch," Ross said.

I'd wanted to believe that she'd gotten clean and was ready for a new life. I knelt down. She looked so peaceful, the only time I'd ever really seen such serenity on her face.

Sometimes you can't save someone from themselves. I

couldn't save Tracy from herself. Neither could Bill nor anyone else.

I reached out and touched her cheek. It was cold. I got up without a word to Ross and walked back outside. I gave one final glance back at the building where any thoughts of renewal and redemption for a lost prodigal child had died in the plastic cylinder of a hypodermic needle. There was nothing more I could do.

I got into my car and drove off into the afternoon heat.

ABOUT THE AUTHOR

RICK NICHOLS has held a deep fascination for Feudal Japan and the code of bushido that guided the samurai since childhood. For Rick, writing was always just a hobby until college, when he got the idea for a character named John Logan—an ex-spy turned private detective. That spurred him to begin to really learn the craft of storytelling.

Rick has served in the U.S. Army as a Military Police-man, and is a graduate of Glenville State College, the Ft Leonard Wood Law Enforcement Academy, and a couple of things that he can't talk about. He holds a belt in *Ko Setumi Sei Kan* karate and has also studied Aikido, Judo, Kung Fu, and even *aki-bujutsu*—the original unarmed combat taught to the ancient samurai.

You can learn more about Rick by going to his website: www.ricknicholsonline.com

Made in the USA
Middletown, DE
07 August 2020

14607563R00151